SECRETS
IN THE KEYS

S.S. DUSKEY

Printed in the United States of America.
First printing, 2020
Cover images by S.S. Duskey & D. Driggers
Cover design and author photo by D. Driggers
Editor Carrie Padgett
Publishing Coordinator – Sharon Kizziah-Holmes

SakiRose Publishing
Hamilton, MT

ssduskey@yahoo.com

ISBN -13: 978-0-578-23662-9

ACKNOWLEDGMENTS

I would like to thank Steve Weinstock, Jon Eubanks, John J. Alvarez, and Teri Albrecht for their expertise, and Charisse Rose for being the best BGD. A special thank-you to Carrie Padgett for her outstanding editing and D. Driggers for the eye-catching cover design and author photo. Lastly, to my family and friends for their unwavering encouragement.

CHAPTER 1

"**D**rop the gun, Jessie!" My heart thumped like a racehorse on his final lap, and my sweat-soaked t-shirt clung to my ballistic vest.

"No ... nope, I can't do that, O'Brien!" He paced and twitched as he waved his stolen Glock 9 mm around in his right hand. His left clutched the dirty denim shorts that hung from his wasted frame.

"I repeat, Silver 288 in need of code 3 cover, does anyone copy?" I pled in my mic as it slipped from my dripping fingers and swung from my raid vest.

"Silver 288, this is dispatch, you ... *tsch* ... what is ... *tsch*." The shriek in my earpiece sent shivers through my body. *Crap, not now.*

"Jess, it's you and me out here. Drop your

weapon so we can talk, no one needs to get hurt." The Sacramento noon heat took its toll as cotton fell out of my mouth instead of words.

"No, man. I can't ... I won't," he sniveled.

Okay, Rose, shoot to stop the threat. During my seven years on the job, I'd never discharged my firearm in the line of duty. It was harder than I'd thought. Just as I removed my finger from the trigger guard, a small crowd of looky-loos gathered. Crap again. They messed with my shot.

"Clear the scene!" I flailed my arm.

They drew closer and swarmed us like bees with their cell phones out. "Call 911!" Nobody dialed. I was in enemy territory. Law enforcement got no help in this part of town. I reached for the mic.

"Don't fucking touch that again," he raged. The chemical odor emitted from his pores. Jessie had been sober for eight months and secured a job as an auto mechanic. What triggered his relapse?

"Okay ... okay." I eased my hand as if slowing traffic and crept to my left, praying for a signal. But the three-story concrete parking garage behind me blocked any hope of communication.

As I swallowed, a lump had taken up residency in my throat. "Jessie, you have my word, I'll put you back in a program." The weight of my full-size Glock 40 loosened from my moist palm. I readjusted my grip.

He stopped pacing. His vacant, worn out, red eyes lowered. "I'm sorry for everything ... I didn't ... it doesn't matter anymore."

Crap, suicide by cop. A vision of tomorrow's headline flashed before me. *Parole Agent Shoots Suicidal Parolee.*

"Jessie, I'm gonna help you. But you need to put down the gun."

"No! You don't get it. I'm fucked either way."

I took a quick peek up and side-stepped left.

Then I heard, "This is dispatch, can anyone get a location on the Silver Unit?" A faint voice crackled. I flinched to answer.

"I told you not to touch that," Jessie yelled through gritted teeth as he wielded the gun at the crowd.

"Easy, Jess." The adrenaline coursed through my body as I hit the red emergency button.

"Dispatch to Silver Unit, what is your location?" I pressed two more times. "All units, we received a distress sign from Silver 288." The dispatcher's voice was cool and even. "GPS coordinates show her in the alley behind Old Branch Rd. All available units respond code three ... keep channels clear."

Beep ... beep ... beep.

My heart pounded in my throat as the priority traffic signal broadcast over the air. I realized how much it sounded like a life-support machine and had often pictured being on this end of the call. I imagined no more.

The scene played out in a slow, muffled motion. As the sirens in the distance grew near, our eyes locked. Tears welled as he raised the Glock. "I'm sorry, Rose. I didn't know he was your husband."

"Wha ...?" I cocked my head.

Pop ... pop ... pop.

CHAPTER 2

I took a Louisville Slugger to the chest while a sizzling dagger seared through my left shoulder. As I gasped for air, I felt flung backward like a rag doll. The summer heat faded as emergency crews rushed toward me. The earsplitting buzzing noise that filled my brain muffled their shouts.

"Shit! Agent down, she's shot. We need an ambulance, now! Get my trauma kit!" A familiar, rattled voice hovered over me, "Rose, stay with me. You have to fi ..."

The world around me gave way, and I was out of my body. I watched paramedics usher my partner away in protest, as they furiously worked to revive my lifeless shell. Sirens continued to wail to the bloody shooting scene, but none of that mattered.

I was at peace.

I became weightless and floated like a feather tossed in the breeze. I traveled through a bright tunnel toward a warm, blissful human-shaped light figure. He was void of distinct facial features.

As I drew closer to Him, two figures emerged and embraced me. I could feel and hear them. They grabbed my hands, and we soared over the most magnificent aromatic rose garden I had ever experienced. The roses were without thorns and caressed my feet. They secreted a sweet scent and were heavenly, vibrant, indescribable colors of red, yellow, purple, pink, and more.

We glided on to a silver bench that was smooth as velvet. I looked right, and Bradley held my hand. His features were blurry, but I knew in my heart it was my love. I glanced left and my mom clung to the other with a tender smile. She wore a white flowing gown and her cascading blonde hair shimmered. *Rosie* ... Oh, how I yearned to hear her say that once more ... *Saki is in danger and needs you.* What did she mean? My sister in danger?

Suddenly, the luminous figure reappeared and communicated to me through my thoughts or a telepathy of sorts. *Rose, my child, it is not your time. You have work ahead of you and must return.*

A quick surge snatched me from their embrace. "No!" I yelped as a painful jolt coursed through me.

"We lost her pulse ... do it again ... clear ..."

My body convulsed. "Okay. Got it. Rose ... Rose ... can you hear me? Ms. O'Brien?" A soothing female voice echoed.

I opened my eyes and was no longer in paradise. I lay shivering on a sterile operating table. My body ached from head to toe.

"Welcome back," she said. She wiped the tears that had fallen down my cheek.

"No, no, please. I don't want to leave." I cried.

She stroked my hand and whispered. "You're not going anywhere. You're gonna be okay."

I was miles from okay. I wasn't even in the same zip code.

CHAPTER 3

Max Ryan started most Sunday mornings on the deck that wrapped-around the entire second floor of his two-story, stylish South Beach condo. He basked shirtless in the Southern Florida heat on his chaise longue and offered his chiseled, tan face to the sun as the ocean mist cooled him. Max allowed himself just a half hour of the morning rays since he intended to avoid the pre-cancerous, pruned faces of those roaming the beaches. As he sipped his cup of imported Italian roasted full-bodied espresso, made with beans from South America and India at a perfect 130 degrees, a smile almost crept in the corner of his mouth.

Max was on his way to obtaining the third painting of a trilogy he'd hunted for sixteen years. Most of the time he got what he wanted. His tactics were less than honorable or legal, but he didn't care. He was as ruthless as the infamous honey badger.

Just as he inhaled the aroma with notes of cocoa powder and smoky molasses, the buzzing of his cell interrupted his olfactory dream. Max squinted at his caller ID.

"You have my package?" he barked. Not a peep from the other end. "I take that as a no?!"

"Uh ... not exactly. There was a slight *hiccup* yesterday," said a male with a strong Bronx accent.

"Dammit, Titos, I don't pay you for *hiccups*. I sent you on one of my jets to do a simple job." He set his coffee on the table and sat straight. "Did you complete it or not?" he demanded.

"The kid's not a problem anymore. But the package hasn't been retrieved yet. I promise, I'll finish the jo—"

"Forget it. Obviously, it's something I need to handle myself." The eerie calm in his voice was the eye of the hurricane.

Max disconnected before he let Titos tell him the rest of his plan and returned to the sun. Just as he closed his eyes, the screen door burst open. Max jumped. He'd forgotten his overnight guest. One of his twenty-something-year-old twinkies emerged from the bedroom, wearing nothing but a bright pink and black lace thong. She stepped behind him and pressed her bare breasts against his back and traced his six-pack abs with her pointy fuchsia acrylic fingernails. She drew a line from nape to his navel.

He slapped her hand away and shot her a sideways glare. She ignored him and draped her freshly dyed extension ginger curls over his shoulders. She turned her attention to his neck and took one long continuous breath. "I love the way you smell. What is that?" she asked in a low raspy whisper.

"It's imported from Italy and designed for me." He kept his view trained on the crashing waves.

She straddled him and twirled her nails around his trimmed chest hair and kissed his neck.

Without missing a beat, Max pushed her off. "I need to make a phone call, Tina. Go get dressed." He waved her away.

She huffed as she dismounted and slammed the screen door. "It's Tiffany, asshole," she snarled, almost under her breath.

Asshole had become his middle name over the years, and he wore it like a badge of honor. He had opened his heart one time in his life. Once was enough.

Max grabbed his phone. "Crockett, fuel the jet. We're leaving for California. I want wheels up by noon." He ended the call and finished his espresso.

CHAPTER 4

H is snoring could have woken the bodies in the morgue.

"Shh. Keep it quiet over there," I mumbled.

Nose-tingling bleach filled the air and machines bleeped. The lighting in my room had warm rose-pink tones, like the sky before sunrise. I blinked a few times and realized I was in the Intensive Care Unit and not on a beach somewhere. In my experience with the ICU, hospitals use circadian lighting to mimic natural light. It worked.

As I adjusted to my new surroundings, I discovered my left shoulder immobilized in a sling and an IV attached to the other arm. I peeked under the pale blue blanket and found a freaking catheter shoved in my bladder. I tried to clear the double vision, but it was useless. I must be drugged up, if my broken body was any indication of my condition.

My attention was re-directed to the snoring that grew louder. I spied a long-legged silhouette outstretched in the corner chair by the window.

"AP, is that you?" I slurred and scanned his dishevelment. His customarily groomed, chestnut brown hair stood straight up like a cockatoo's feather, and his mouth hung open as his mustache wiggled to the vibration. AP was the nickname I gave my best friend and work partner, but James Powers was his given name. He called me Felicity.

"Wha ... oh, you're awake." He yawned and stretched.

"Hey, partner. What happened? Where am I, how long have I be ...?" I reached for my bed remote. "Ahh ... holy crap!"

"Eeeasy, there. Let me help." He bolted up from the chair.

"I got it." I cleared my throat and winced.

"Stubborn brat. You never need help, do you?" he whispered and raised my bed. "It's Sunday morning. You're at Mercy and you were shot yesterday." He responded matter-of-factly.

"What?" I furrowed my brows.

"Uh ... the answer to your questions," he replied.

"Sorry, James. Have you been here the whole time?"

"I wouldn't leave until you woke up ... that's what partners do." He gave a closed mouth grin as he towered over me.

"Thank you, but I'm fine now. You need to go home and get rest, you're grumpy and—" I glimpsed his red-splattered shirt. "Is that my blood?"

He nodded. "You should see my button down, it's soaked. I used it to stop your bleeding."

"Sorry." I lowered my gaze.

"Whoa, wait a minute." He held his hand like a traffic cop. "I should be the one to say sorry. I wasn't there, but ..." He let out an exaggerated sigh. "I, we, your partners, didn't know where you were." He crossed his arms.

"I ... I received a call about Jessie, and he wanted to—"

"Agent O'Brien, when are you gonna bring me in on these tips?"

"Oh, Agent O'Brien is it? Look, it was not a tip. Jessie was ready to turn himself in to me. If he saw the team, he would've got a little rabbit in him. Besides, I texted you and my supervisor the location."

"Yeah, I got your text ..." He air quoted. "That's not effective communication. Do you remember when your agency joined our task force a year ago? The emphasis was on teamwork. You're not a one-woman crusade. That's reckless and dangerous, you know better than that."

"Really? You're gonna lecture me now?" I looked to the ceiling.

He exhaled. "You're right. I'll chew your ass out when you're released." James's voice softened, and he held my hand. "But seriously. I love you like a sister and I promised Brad, I'd watch out for you."

"Speaking of Brad ... I had a weird dream, at least I think it was a dream. He and my mom were there and ... you're gonna think I'm crazy, but ... God spoke to me ..." I shivered. "I don't know, must be all the medi—" I shook my head. "What's that look for? Oh, great, you do think I'm nuts."

"Well." His face scrunched. "It may not have been a dream. When I arrived on scene, you didn't have a pulse. You also coded while in surgery ... Felicity, we lost you twice." James wiped a tear with his shoulder. "I must have something in my eye." He walked into the bathroom.

As I reflected on my experience, I realized someone was missing. "Hey! James, where's Saki?!"

CHAPTER 5

"James! Where is my sister? Where is Saki?!" My heart pounded as I threw off the sheets and planted a foot. "I have to find her!" The room spun, and I fell back as quick as I stood. My monitor alerted as if I were an escaped convict.

"Whoa!" James bolted and caught me before I hit the floor. "She's getting breakfa—"

A short, reddish-brown haired RN burst in and shoved James out of the way. "Excuse me, sir." She fired a nasty glare at my partner. He opened his mouth, but she'd just started her lecture. "You can't get up on your own yet, Rose."

James's six-foot frame towered over her petite stature. His big, round brown eyes stared at me as if he were a child caught stealing candy. He stood behind her and brushed one index finger across the top of the other, the universal sign for *naughty, naughty*.

She whirled around with her hands on her hips. "Make sure she stays in that bed!" she barked at him.

James bent forward, read her name tag, and saluted. "Aye, aye, Ms. Scarlett."

She scowled as she scanned him, but her facial expression softened when her eyes met the blood splatter on his shirt.

Scarlett returned to me and retrieved a syringe from her navy-blue smock covered in dachshund puppies and injected it into my IV. Before I asked what she was giving me, it no longer mattered. The pain was gone, and I felt groovy. "You need to take it easy, my dear," she said, her tone soothing. She tapped on the IV line and jiggled the catheter bag. "Ask for help the next time you want out of bed."

AP shot me an *I told you so look* over her. "She doesn't know how to ask for help." He smirked.

I blew him a half-hearted raspberry as Scarlett sauntered past him.

"And ..." She waved a flirty finger at him. "You need to behave, mister. I'm watching you."

"Oh, I will behave," he said, his voice low and deep. He snarled with his face and made eye contact with her until she left.

I braced for what was coming next. He turned to me. "Yeah, baby. Oh behave." The Austin Powers' theme song played in my brain as he pranced back to his sleeping chair. He leaned over and shook his butt at me and peeked over one shoulder and then the other as he put his pinky to his lip.

I lost it and let out a huge snort laugh. Life returned to normal for a moment.

"Now that's music to my ears." A friendly voice interrupted our fun.

CHAPTER 6

Saki stood in the doorway laughing, holding a brown paper sack. She wore a flowing, white cotton halter dress, and her golden locks cascaded over tan shoulders. I forgot how much she resembled our father. They shared the same athletic, lean body and contagious smile that lit up any room. Saki was the runt of the litter at five foot five inches, while Dad topped six feet by a couple of inches.

My partner stopped in mid-dance with his butt high in the air and quickly turned around, red-faced. He cleared his throat, smoothed his hair, and adjusted his shirt. James gazed at her, speechless with a twinkle in his eyes I had not seen since before his divorce.

"Baby sister!" I beamed.

"Good morning, Rosie ... oops, Rose." She

wrinkled her nose. Only our mother called me that, but I let it slide. "I'm sooo glad you're awake!" She squealed as she set the food on the table and ran to my bedside. She buried her face in my shoulder. "I —I— don't know what I'd do without you." She sobbed.

"I'm here, honey, I'm not going anywhere." I whimpered as pain radiated through my body. But I didn't care, my baby sister was in my arms.

"O.M.G., I am so sorry." She loosened her Star Wars death grip on me. "You are totally tore up and here I am squeezing the shit out of you!" She responded in her unfiltered, profane way.

James grabbed his breakfast and tip-toed toward the exit during our teary-eyed reunion.

"Um, where are you going ... Mr. Powers?" She giggled and turned to him.

"Okay, I'm embarrassed. It's called lack of sleep." He waved his burrito and took a bite. "Thanks."

"Aww, thanks for coming see me." I tossed off the sheet and swayed as I planted both feet on the floor.

They rushed to me. "What the hell are you doing?" Saki scolded.

"Ready go home." I slurred and leaned backward.

"Not so quick, sweetheart," Saki said.

They reached me at the same time and grazed one another's hands as they lowered me back in bed. James took a wrong turn and got lost in her azure blue eyes.

"You keep your ass in bed. You just had surgery yesterday." Saki snarled at me.

"Um ... yep, listen to your sister, Felicity. You need to be here longer."

"Yeah right, that's na gonna happen." I snorted. I thought it was an internal statement.

"Oh, boy," they responded in unison.

"Okay, Okay, k, k ..."

They stared quietly at me as I mumbled. Saki, normally a chatter box, bit her lip at the stillness of the room. "Hey, now I know why you call her Felicity and your AP. It's the whole Austin Powers thing ... yeah ..." She let out a puff of air as she looked around.

"It's kind of our thing ... long story. Um, I should leave. I think you can take it from here." James turned. "Oh, thanks again for breakfast."

Saki tilted her head sideways and completed her full body scan as James strutted out the door.

"Where have you been hiding him, sis?" she whispered.

"He's my bess frien." I closed my eyes.

"Get some rest, Rosie. I love you." She giggled and patted my hand.

I drifted off with a mumbled, "Love you more."

CHAPTER 7

Max reclined in his 2017 Gulf Stream G450 and savored his gin martini with a splash of vermouth. He stroked the soft leather tan seats with walnut veneer trim and gazed out at the clouds as they passed. His jet was the epitome of luxury with its twin Rolls-Royce engines. It optimized fresh air circulation and low cabin pressure to reduce in-flight fatigue. The Stream had oval windows for extra natural light, three living areas that slept up to six people, two bathrooms, and a full galley.

He lifted his empty glass and motioned for the flight attendant to bring him his second martini. *Another new girl?* He raised a freshly groomed eyebrow. Crockett was not only his pilot, but his right-hand man and in charge of the hiring, so Max didn't bother to remember their names.

Just as she refreshed his drink, the phone rang.

"What, Titos?"

"Boss, there's a newspaper article you need to read."

"Why?"

"You'll see, sending it to you now."

Parole Agent, Rose O'Brien, with the Department of Corrections was shot Saturday afternoon when she encountered wanted parolee, Jessie Jones. The shooting occurred shortly after noon ... blah, blah, blah. Parolee succumbed to his injuries. Agent O'Brien was critically wounded in an exchange of gunfire and is recovering in a local hospital ...

Max scrolled through the article, and his heart skipped a beat. Hearing her name was one thing, but seeing her picture was another. Her golden, red-silky hair, flawless, shimmering skin, and blue eyes the color of sapphires, with an unforgettable smile. He lamented for a moment at what could have been. But her face mocked him and stirred an emotion he hadn't felt in twenty-three years. He quickly replied with a text:

Max: *FIND HER LOCATION!*

Titos: *Faith Mercy.*

He threw the phone on the chair across from him, drew a deep breath and gulped his drink. A tidal wave of anger surged. Max had everything under control, or so he thought. He snapped his fingers and raised his glass. After his third drink, he reclined, put his eye mask on and drifted to sleep.

CHAPTER 8

A giant ogre of a man wearing black slacks and a white-collared shirt with whiskey on his breath yanked him down a steep, dark concrete stairwell. He kicked and screamed, but his voice couldn't pass his lips. The man threw him on the cold, concrete floor of a padded room without windows. As he turned, the door locked behind him. The ogre stood between him and freedom. As he shivered in the corner, the beatings continued.

"No! Please, stop. Go away." He moaned and thrashed. His clothes were wet with fear.

A hand on his arm shook him, and a voice pierced the terror. "Mr. Ryan, wake up. Sir."

Max's eyes flew open. He snatched the flight attendant's arm, squeezing it until her fingers turned white.

"Ow, you're hurting me!"

He quickly released his clutch and glared at her. "Don't ever touch me again. Do you understand?" He spoke in a slow, deliberate tone.

She took a few steps back, rubbing her arm, her gaze locked on his, and nodded.

He sat upright, straightened his tousled hair, and fixed his tie. She stood with her mouth open.

"What?" he snapped.

"Um … nothing?" She spun around to walk away, stopped, and turned back. "Oh, yeah." She shook her head. "Crockett informed me we'll be landing in twenty minutes."

"Fine, you can go now." He dismissed her with a flick of his hand. "Oh, get me water and an aspirin."

As she made her way to the galley, she massaged her arm and mumbled. "Not even a sorry or a thank-you? What a weird asshole. I'm returning to the airlines." She turned back to him and furrowed her brows.

Max glared back and waited until she was out of sight to retrieve his briefcase. He pulled out a thick black rubber band. "I haven't had to use this in a while." He placed it on his left wrist. Max closed his eyes, drew a deep breath, and gave it a sharp snap, then another. He repeated this several times until his wrist reddened with pain.

CHAPTER 9

While the ballistic vest saved my life, the energy from the lethal impact had to go somewhere. I suffered cracked ribs, a bruised clavicle, and underwent surgery to remove the bullet lodged in my shoulder. Some would say I was lucky. If Jessie had a higher caliber than a 9 mm, I would be dead.

What did Jessie want to tell me? Why did he apologize? How did he know Bradley? I was deep in thought and did not hear anyone enter.

"Ahem." James cleared his throat. "Earth to Agent O'Brien."

I shot him a fake grin.

"Boy, you were out there." He walked over and kissed my forehead.

"Sooo, how is my favorite FBI Agent and the best partner in the whole wide world?" I asked.

His eyes widened. "Ha, someone is still on some excellent shit."

"What?" I frowned.

"You were in another realm and mumbling."

"Nope, no more narcotics, only Motrin. I'm feeling better and ready to leave." I fibbed, but hospitals were the worst. I'd spent my fair share of them in the cancer ward with my mother.

"Hey, they just moved you to the penthouse suite." James motioned to my room. "No, seriously love, it's only been two days. I spoke to the doc, and it looks like you'll be here another week, or so."

I snickered.

"Don't be a stubborn brat, you almost died!"

I shrugged and grimaced. "What can I say, it's something I'm good at ... so, what's up buttercup?" I watched as he perused my room filled with flowers and get-well cards, some from total strangers.

He stopped at one arrangement and stared. The bouquet had four roses. A large red rose surrounded by smaller yellow, pink, and orange ones. "These are unique," he said.

"Yeah, I didn't see those." I sat up straighter. "Who sent them?"

"No card."

"Hmm, my dad used to ... nah that's impossible ... never mind," I said.

He crossed his arms and stood at the foot of my bed.

"AP, I know you didn't come here to chat about flowers. You're doing that lip biting thing. Spill it."

Just then two armed agents stepped in and nodded at my partner. I recognized one from my department, the other was an FBI agent I'd met once during a field op. James held his hand to them. "Let me brief Agent O'Brien first." They exited and posted outside the open door.

"Brief me on what? What the heck is going on?" My stomach churned. "Am I in trouble ... shouldn't my union rep be here?"

"No, the opposite." He sighed and bit his lower lip again. "You may have been the target."

CHAPTER 10

"**W**hat are you talking about?" I frowned. "Me? The target? That's crazy!"

"You guys were not alone out there, Rose. There was a party crasher. Someone shot Jessie in the melon using a subsonic .300 Blackout." James pulled up a chair and sat beside me. "The shooter was sloppy and left a shell casing."

"But ... I would have heard a .300 whizzing past me. I've been thinking, and I'm positive I fired my weapon. Besides, why would the Highway Patrol have taken it for their investigation?" I rubbed my shoulder and stared straight ahead, running through the scene in my head yet again.

"The gunman must have used a suppressor.

And you're correct, you shot Jessie center mass, but a preliminary autopsy showed the .300 hit him first, in the noggin. Practically took it clean off, it was a messy scene." James shuddered and shook his head, as if that would erase the gruesome image from his brain.

"Okay, Mr. I-have-an-answer-for-everything. If there was a bullseye on me, why am I still here? The shooter was obviously a pro, why did he or she miss me?" I swung my feet over the side of the bed. "And what are they doing here?" I stood and jutted my chin at the agents posted.

"Easy, tiger ..." James blocked me as his phone buzzed with an incoming text. "Shit! I didn't want to alarm you until we got confirmation." He closed the door. "They—" he nodded to the agents— "are here for your protection. The Crime Scene Investigators just completed their work-up on a black duffle bag found near the scene. The local CSI just advised me it contained a syringe of Ketamine, duct tape, rope, and black gloves." James looked at me. "You weren't shot because you were the target of a kidnapping." He paced like a worried father, waiting for his daughter to return from her first date.

"What the hell? Why me? And what was Jessie's involvement?" I quivered.

"Look." He sat on the edge of my bed. "You said you'd received an anonymous call. What did the caller sound like? Male or female?" He drew out a pad from his shirt pocket and took notes as if he were interviewing a victim.

Which I suppose he was. But I didn't have to like it.

"I told you, it was an unknown number. He had an East Coast accent," I snapped.

"Considering the recent evidence, you're getting increased security."

"Come on Powers, I don't need a freaking babysitter. I can take care of myself!"

"Don't get cross with me, young lady." He sprang to his feet and loomed over my bed. "Agent O'Brien, it's not your choice, there are two departments involved. Don't be a hero! Look at you! You were shot two days ago, you only have one functioning arm, bruised ribs, and a hole in your shoulder. I'll bet you can't even wipe your own ass!"

We stared at one another then burst into laughter at the absurdity of his last comment.

"All right, AP," I replied. My words agreed with him, but they were hollow.

He glanced at his watch. "It's getting late and I have paperwork to finish. Get some rest. I'll come by in the morning." He turned back. "If you need *anything*, call me. I don't care the time. I love you, Brat."

Among many nicknames, *Brat* was his favorite when he thought I was too difficult.

"I love you, too." I flashed a cheeky grin. As he closed the door, I gazed around at the love and warmth in the get-well cards and flowers that filled my room. But I couldn't shake the quiet uneasiness that enveloped me like an approaching slow-moving winter's storm.

CHAPTER 11

He roamed the halls of the hospital, trying to glimpse patients in beds or names or visitors. Anything to identify who was in the room. Finally, he approached a mousy-haired RN in her sixties who sat behind the nurses' station typing into a computer.

"May I help you?" she asked flatly without looking up.

"Good evening, young lady." Max was the perfect chiseled specimen of a man at six feet, three inches tall, a slim one hundred eighty pounds, raven black hair, cerulean eyes, and sun-kissed skin.

She looked up and blinked. "H—hi ... I'm Tonie." She pulled her name tag toward him as she stood. "How ... how can you help me?" She blushed and giggled. "I mean how can I help you?" Tonie drew a long deep breath and closed her eyes.

Max waited at the counter until she returned from Aromaville. He cleared his throat.

"Uh ... my apologies it's been a long night and your cologne ... it's heavenly." She batted her fake eyelashes.

A doctor approached and grabbed a chart.

Tonie stood tall, pressed her smock, and tucked her hair in her bun. "I'm sorry sir, is there something you need?" She spoke loudly until the doctor walked away.

"Yes, you can, beautiful. My name is Max Ryan. I just arrived from back east on my private jet. I was hoping to see my cousin. She's the agent who was wounded in the line of duty." He shot her a model's toothy smile.

"Your ... your jet?" She rested her chin on her hand and gawked like a starstruck schoolgirl. "Wow!"

Women always threw themselves at Max, and he didn't have to work for it. Back in college, his friends nicknamed him PD for pantie-dropper. "Yes. I am here on a quick business trip and would like to check on Rose Rea—I mean, Rose O'Brien."

Tonie peered at her clipboard. "Mr. Ryan, sir, your name is not on the list. I have strict orders prohibiting unauthorized visitors. I'm so sorry."

Max let out a heavy sigh as his ears burned. He had to stay calm and could not use his normal tactics, like choking the information out of her. So, PD to the job. He leaned close and whispered in her ear. "Have you ever made love on a private jet?"

Tonie dragged her head backward and slowly shook it.

Max bent over far enough to get what he needed. *R. O'Neil, Room 220.* "Thanks anyway, Tasha." He waved his hand in a dismissal fashion.

She trained her eyes on him and her mouth hung open. "It's Tonie. Wha ... what about your question?" Her voice trailed as he walked out of sight.

As Max slithered around the corner, he spotted a stocky armed agent standing guard in front of Room 220. Max nodded at him and continued past. Soon.

CHAPTER 12

*H*i Rose Bud, I'm back. James dropped *me off at the auto shop. I can't wait to tell you about the visit.*

Welcome back, I missed you honey. What did you find out? How is he? Never mind, tell me when you get home. But drive safe, the roads are a mess. Take Eagle Point, Pine is washed out. I love you.

I love you too, my little rosebud ... Rose ... Rose, wake up.

"Wha ..." I jolted and shot my eyes open. Somebody called my name. I squinted and blinked a few times to focus. The only illumination came from the flashing heart monitor and my clock that read midnight.

Okay Rose, it's just a dream, Bradley's not here. I exhaled a loud whoosh when suddenly the privacy curtain moved. "Hello, hello? Is someone there? Nurse?" It moved again, and a tall figure vanished in the shadows. My heart palpitated.

I shuffled out of bed and yanked back the curtain, but no one was there. I noticed the door ajar and instantly caught the whiff of a man's cologne. At the hall, I peered to the left, but there was no sign of anyone. As I turned to the right, I jumped.

"Whoa. What the hell?" I shrieked. "You scared the crap out of me." I stood nose to belly with a ginormous man. My eyes met his waist, and I spied his gun and badge. I scanned upward and found a baby-faced kid.

"I'm sorry, Agent O'Brien. Is everything okay?"

"I'm fine, but were you in my room?"

"No, ma'am, I just came on duty. We were conducting our shift briefing, and I saw your door open. Maybe it was the night nurse." He towered over me. "Uh, since you're awake, I'd like to say you rocked it out there and held your own. If you need anything, I am on till eight." He extended his hand. "Agent Thomas Riley."

"Thanks, Riley." I reciprocated. "I'm going back to my room now. Hey, I thought there were two agents? Where are the feds?"

He shrugged. "Don't know. It was only our department when I came on tonight. Get some rest and feel better soon. I look forward to seeing you out there and maybe working with you sometime."

I nodded and shut the door. Agent Riley

wanted to discuss the shooting and live vicariously through me, but that was the last thing on my mind. As I re-entered my room, I walked through the lingering fog of my intruder's cologne. It occurred to me, *nurses are forbidden to wear any fragrance.* My body trembled. *Someone was here.*

CHAPTER 13

I remained vigilant the rest of the morning and called an Uber after the nurse finished her five a.m. rounds. Agent Riley was still on duty when I peeked my head out. He reassured me I had no unauthorized visitors. I knew that was BS. I shut my mouth and nodded a thank-you. He further advised that the feds were on point outside, which made my escape challenging.

Just as I closed my door, the Uber driver texted he was ten minutes out. I said I needed fifteen and to meet me out back. He didn't ask questions and obliged my request. Time was ticking, and I had to evade two departments' captors.

The solution hit me. I peeked out again and told Riley I had female problems and had to walk off my cramps. He stammered and looked around and that's when he spotted Rachel changing a bedpan in the next room. She was a green nurse's aide, maybe three days on the job and eager to help. Okay, first part of the plan complete.

Riley agreed to let us stroll the wing but trailed close behind, avoiding eye contact. I breathed a sigh of relief when a Code Blue on the floor sent the staff scrambling. Riley lifted his eyes off me a second as Rachel split to assist. That was my cue.

I'd reached an all-time low, or so I thought, taking advantage of another's health crisis to flee. My adrenaline raced as I slipped out the exit door and bolted downstairs. I didn't feel pain until I jumped in the back seat of my driver's car.

By his profile, his name was Terrance, and he was every bit handsome as he was young. He must have been Saki's age. He had toffee brown cropped cut hair, hazel eyes, a small goatee, and broad shoulders. As I slammed the door, I told Terrance to burn rubber and kept looking back as we sped away.

CHAPTER 14

Terrance spent more time looking in the rear-view mirror than on the road ahead as my moans from the backseat grew louder. He turned and asked if I needed to return to Mercy.

"I'm good, just keep driving." My pasty white grimacing face was probably not believable, not to mention the faded oversized blue hospital gown hanging off my shoulder, revealing dried blood. I was the poster child for the ER.

As we hit the I-5 freeway, I caught him gawking again. "Forgive me, but have we met?"

I shook my head.

He snapped his fingers. "Oh, yeah, now I know. You're that parole agent, I saw you in the paper and the news. You are kind of a big deal." He sat up straighter in his seat, as if he were the proud Uber driver for a celebrity.

I gave him a closed mouth, fake smile. "Hey, Terrance. Please don't tell anyone I was in your car or where you're taking me."

He nodded. "Sure thing. Can I ask you a question?"

I leaned against the headrest and mumbled. "Mmm hmm." He held me captive, I had no choice but to be cordial.

"How did it feel? You know, getting shot."

"What I remember, it hurt like a son of a bitch." I shut my eyes and prayed for silence. Just then my cell buzzed in my hand. Before I looked at the caller ID, I knew it had to be one of two people. I drew a deep breath and braced for the lecture.

"Hey, boss." I rolled my eyes during the five-minute butt chewing. Amy Puckett, my first-line supervisor, was a by the book hard-ass. She ranted without surfacing for air. I was reckless leaving Against Medical Advice, she said, or A.M.A. It's only been three days, I took a risk, they still don't know who shot me, yada, yada, yada.

Her dissertation magnified the pounding in my skull. I pulled the phone away from my ear and jerked my back. "Okay, look, I'm a grown ass woman and can take care of myself!"

I regretted it the second it spewed from my mouth. "I'm sorry, Amy. I'm not a fan of hospitals, especially the trauma unit. They're a breeding ground for diseases, and I'm positive half my caseload was in there. Besides, I couldn't get any sleep. I'm better off at home."

I wanted to tell her the truth. The hospital wasn't safe and whoever targeted me had penetrated the security detail, but I left that part out.

"Can we compromise? I'll follow up with my doctor and have my wounds checked daily and ... oh, come on ... I don't need a bloody sitter." I released a loud puff of air. "Okay, fine. The squad can sit on my house, under one condition ... yes, unmarked, and undercover. Thank you!"

I hung up and peered back to make sure we weren't being followed. I didn't breathe until we started our ascent to Grass Valley, my safe place.

Or so I thought.

CHAPTER 15

The late afternoon sun blinded him as he sat in his rented black Escalade and peered through his Bushnell binoculars. Rose lived in a heavily wooded section of Grass Valley, and surveillance on his unsuspecting prey posed a challenge. He positioned himself two rural blocks away as to not raise any suspicions.

Her residence was smaller than the rest of her neighbors on what appeared to be half an acre. Her tan and brown ranch-style home was modest. Most of the adjoining lots were at least two acres, and somewhere in the mid five to six hundred thousand range. I could have given you so much more, he mused.

As he scanned the outer perimeter of her house, he observed them. The agents were sitting in Chevy trucks on both sides of the street, one posted outside her front door.

He snatched up his phone and dialed. "Titos, I thought you were getting the watch dogs called off!" he snapped.

"Hey, ya think it's that simple? I don't have a freakin' magic wand!"

Max lowered his voice. "Do not use that tone with me. I could make you disappear, and nobody would know or even give a damn. If you did your job, I would not be here, cleaning up your mess," Max retorted.

"I'm working on it, but I ain't makin' any promises. The feds were one thing, but I'm not sure about her department. Ya know, I been meaning to ask, why the hell are ya here? You've got plenty of West Coast grunts to do your dirty work."

"Some things you have to do for yourself, this is one of them." He raised his eyebrow. "I want them gone. I don't care how, just do it." Max ended the call.

His confidence in Titos waned. He needed a Plan B.

An hour later a yellow, late model Toyota Corolla pulled up and interrupted his thoughts. A blonde girl exited the vehicle and entered the house using a key.

"Hmm, roommate?" He asked out loud as he zoomed in with his Bushnell. "No, is that her ..."

Max jumped at the buzzing from an incoming text:

Titos: *It's done, but not till tomorrow.*

He set the binoculars on his lap and smirked. "Plan B just arrived."

CHAPTER 16

"It's six fifteen, where is she?" I paced in front of the window. "Don't panic, Rose." Of course, I panicked, Saki was always home by five thirty. She moved in with me three months ago when Bradley died. We had a mutual agreement, if either of us were late, we would call or text. Saki obliged my incessant need for her to check in with me, she called me *smotherly*.

As I glanced outside for the tenth time, I found it peculiar that my security detail was gone without an explanation after only one day of surveillance. Although they were no longer posted, an eerie chill settled over me as if he were watching. Did he know where we lived? My mother's warning resonated in my mind. But if Saki was in danger, why was I targeted?

I phoned her again, but it went straight to voice mail. Crap, if she does not come home soon I ...

The door opened and Saki entered, already rambling. "Oh my God, sooo sorry, sis! My phone went dead, and I couldn't find my charger. Please don't be ma—"

I ran to her and gave her a one-armed bear hug.

"Whoa. It's all right, Rose."

I wiped a tear I hid from her. "I was worried. The roads are ... and your car is a piece of garbage." I swallowed a sob.

Her mouth dropped as I fell apart.

"Saki, you are my entire world and I'd never forgive myself if anything happened." I continued to blubber.

"Rose." She stopped me in mid rant. "I'm here. I know these streets can be hairy with the sudden rain. I won't drive off the hill like—" My facial expression told her we were not ready to go there.

"Okay, sorry, I'm fine." I said with a forged smile.

"I am sure you are just F.I.N.E., fine." She giggled.

"Hey, I am not f'd up, insecure, neurotic, and emotional."

"Seriously Rose, you still can't say fuck?" She snickered again as she flung her sneakers in the entry.

"I regret telling you what that means, Ms. Potty Mouth. Now that you're here safe, I'm going to take a hot bath," I said over my shoulder as I made my way down the hall. "And put your shoes away. I'm not your bloody maid."

"Okay, okay ... hey, I'm starved, gonna order a pizza."

"Sounds good!" An ease came over me for the moment.

CHAPTER 17

He sat in his second SUV rental in two days. Although Titos had the dogs called off that afternoon, Max didn't want to risk being recognized. He parked across the street and pondered Plan B. Just then a white Subaru with a Dominos magnetic sign on the roof pulled up to the house.

"Can this get any easier?" He wore a smug grin as he exited his vehicle.

He dashed to the car and put on his happy face as he approached the pubescent delivery boy. "Hey man. Perfect timing, I can take that from you. Don't want you to get wet." Max grabbed the pizza and gave him a fifty. "Here you go, keep the change."

"Wow! Thanks dude, you made my week." The kid burned rubber before his generous tipper changed his mind.

Max waited until the kid left before he approached her residence. The door flung open as he rang the bell. His heart skipped a beat. *She's the spitting image of her father*. He shook it off. He had work to do.

"Hi!" Saki said with a wide smile. "Come in out of the rain." She bounced as she ushered him inside. She obviously had just pizza on the brain and didn't notice he was too old to be a pizza delivery guy. Or that his Prada polo shirt with matching jeans, and Berluti Loafers, wasn't usual attire for a minimum wage worker. Hell, his entire ensemble cost more than her car.

What she detected as she turned to hand him his money, was his cologne. She closed her eyes and drew a deep breath. "Wow, I don't know what smells better, you or the pepperoni, mushroom, garlic, and cheese pizza."

Saki stared at him, took the box, and handed him a piece of paper. They both looked at it. "Uh, sorry, let me get you cash." She giggled.

He knew he had that effect on women. *PD on the job*, he snickered to himself.

As she turned to retrieve her wallet, Max spotted their five-foot-tall Lance gun safe in the living room. He made a mental note as he scanned the rest of the house.

The kitchen had green swirled granite counter tops and cherry wood cabinets. Their immaculate home was furnished in contemporary modern Italian furniture. The Realtor.com search displayed pictures before the remodel. *Humph, fair job on the remodel, for middle class.*

As he looked down the hall, he spotted the master bedroom. On the opposite side of the house were two more bedrooms and a bathroom. The rear sliding door behind the dining room went out to a covered patio that backed to a densely forested hillside.

"All this pizza just for you?" He shot her his winningest smile.

"Nooo. It's for me and my sister. She's taking a bath." Saki had no filter and talked to strangers, especially hot ones.

"How does someone as slim as you eat pizza?" He scanned her and thought, *if you were not Plan B.*

She caught him checking her out and turned pink. "My name is Saki." She gushed as she extended her hand to shake his. I'm a trainer at Fit One, in Auburn."

"That's right, Saki," he said.

"Huh?" She cocked her head like a puppy.

"I mean it's such a rare name." He recovered his fumble.

"Yeah, I get that a lot. My dad was a fan of the British writer."

He ignored her remark of her father. He couldn't afford to lose focus. "I'm new in town. I've been thinking of joining a gym."

She gave the farm away. She told him when and where she worked. She even offered to give him a personal tour.

Max watched her chatter away. When the bathroom door opened, she turned with money still in her hands, and he was gone in an instant.

"It's like taking candy from a baby." He sneered as he dashed to his vehicle.

Max throbbed with adrenaline. It had been over ten years since he'd been in the trenches and gotten his hands dirty.

CHAPTER 18

I stepped out of the bathroom. While soaking in the tub, I'd decided to tell Saki the truth. Before our mother died six months ago, we'd planned on telling her the sordid family secrets. But my sister didn't cope well with trauma and we'd put it off. Three months later tragedy hit again when Bradley was killed. Timing was never right, except tonight, or so I thought.

"Hey, Sak, can we talk ..." Nausea overwhelmed my stomach. *No!* The same men's cologne that lingered in my hospital room was now in my home.

"Saki!" I ran to the kitchen counter. "Who was here?" I barked.

"Pisha guy." She mumbled with a mouth full

of food as she nodded to the door. "Sorry, I was starved and ..." Saki's eyes followed me as I ping-ponged around the house.

"When did he leave? What did he look like?" I interrogated her as I dashed out shoeless and in a robe. I tripped to the end of the sidewalk and watched a white Escalade screech away.

I bolted back inside, jotted the license plate, and dropped next to her. "Saki, honey." I drew a deep breath. "Describe him to me."

"Rose, he's just a delivery boy, or, uh, sexy man." She raised her eyebrows and shimmied her shoulders. "He smelled so yummy."

"What did he say? What did you say ... you didn't give him your number, did you?" I peppered her with questions. My sister had a weakness for good looking men and passed her digits out like Halloween candy.

"Of course not, silly. I invited him on a tour of the gym. I think he was into me." She grinned ear to ear and took another bite.

"You shouldn't have done that." I slapped my forehead.

"Rosie, you're scaring me." Her smile faded. "What the hell is going on?"

"Nothing, sweetie. I'm not myself." I patted her arm and went to my bedroom. I didn't want to alarm her and so sheltered her from awful things.

Our family story would have to wait another night.

I called James, but I went right to voice mail. "Crap... hey, it's me. I need a plate run. Queen X-ray Robert 123. Someone was here."

CHAPTER 19

M ax watched Saki bounce out of the house at five a.m. on the dot. She wore form fitting black yoga pants and a pink tankini with a white unzipped sweatshirt with *Fit One* on the back.

"Punctual girl," he said as he followed her the five miles to Java Hut. Why didn't her tires go flat though? He'd sliced them deep enough.

Finally. As she drove the windy road, one tire blew out, and then another until she fishtailed into the ditch. He grinned.

The sun ascended on the horizon and he needed to strike before more cars were on the highway.

"Here we go, Mr. Knight-in-Shining-Armor." Max pulled up behind her Toyota. He jumped out and opened the rear passenger door to his

SUV.

Saki pushed her own door open and stood on the side of the road, staring at her car, perched in the ditch with two flat tires.

"Are you okay, miss?" he asked.

"Shit! Just what I needed." Saki turned around. "Oh, hi!" She gave him a radiant smile. "The pizza guy from last night, right? What a strange coincidence. I'm sorry, I don't remember your name."

"It's Max." He tried to hide his grin as he stood beside her. "Some luck, huh? I'll call a tow." He patted his pockets. "Darn, left it at home."

"That's all right, I'll use mine. After all it's my car." She removed her cell from the side pocket of her yoga pants.

"Here, let's get you off the road before you're hit." He escorted her to the rear passenger side of the Escalade and glanced at her code as she unlocked the phone.

A truck appeared round the corner. Max grit his teeth. Saki swiped and tapped the phone, searching for a tow company. Finally, the truck passed. He grabbed the needle from the front seat, put his left hand over her mouth while he jabbed her neck with his right, and lifted her into the car.

"What the hell ..." She melted into the backseat.

He grabbed her phone, shut the door, and jumped in the driver's side. As he sped away, he made his own call. "Titos, I got her. The car needs a push, it's on the corner of Oat and

Maple. You can't miss it. When you're finished, hit the house. The safe first."

CHAPTER 20

I jolted awake and groped for my phone. "Crap! It's six o'clock. How did I sleep through the alarm?" My body throbbed as I scrambled out of bed.

"Saki!" I raced to her room. "I need you to stay home today. I have a doctor's appointment." I didn't, but it was the best I could come up with to keep her with me. "You have to take me ..." Her room was empty. I dashed to the kitchen. Also empty. Then I went to the front window to check the driveway. Her car was gone. Damn. She'd already left.

I phoned her, but it went to voice mail. I called the gym and was told she hadn't made it in yet.

So, I did what any rational person would do. I stuffed my gun in my purse and sped off, not realizing I was in my pajamas. I drove her route to work, looking for her Toyota. I prayed she just had car problems. But there were no signs of her.

I zipped into the gym parking lot and jumped out, leaving my car running. As I ran into Janis' office, I couldn't catch my breath. "Is Sa ... Saki here yet?"

Janis was Saki's boss, and at thirty looked twenty.

"No, and that's unusual ... but are you all right, Rose?" She lowered her laptop screen and studied me over her Gucci computer glasses. "You look, um, not yourself."

A crazy-haired, fast-talking street urchin stared at me in the mirror behind Janis. It took a second to realize I was her. My unbrushed hair hung in a half-assed sideways ponytail, my bloody stained sling fell loosely around my shoulder, and I had shopping bags under my eyes. Oh, and the icing was my mismatched Wonder Woman jammie top and Supergirl bottoms. Janis was right. I was not myself and had no clue where she went. All that mattered was finding Saki.

"No, I'm not okay. When Saki gets here, have her call me immediately, please."

Janis said she would, offered me coffee and a hairbrush, but I declined.

As I sped home, I took Eagle Point and scoured both sides of the road. My tires squealed at every windy turn. I shuddered at the thought of my baby sister meeting her end in a fiery crash like Bradley. *This is all my fault. Why did I have to sleep?* I was a pro at shoulda, coulda, woulda scenarios.

An intense burning pain stabbed my heart. *Something's wrong.*

CHAPTER 21

Just as Max pulled up to the Auburn airport, his cell phone buzzed. "Is it done?" he snapped.

"I took care of the car, but not the house."

"And you call yourself a professional?"

"Fuck off! Some guy showed up. I barely got out the side door before he ... ah, damn it, I left the ram ... I never work this sloppy. It's all your fault, you arrogant son of a bi—"

"*Don't*. Don't you dare finish that sentence ... so help me!" he said through gritted teeth. "Never, ever call me that or even think about speaking to me that way." The veins bulged in his neck.

"I quit. Do your own fuckin' dirty work. I don't need this from you. I got a job."

Max drew a deep, deliberate breath and

peered in the back at his drugged victim. He needed Titos at this moment. "I'm sure your employer would be happy to know that you are on my payroll too." He spoke with a calm, eerie tone. Silence fell on the line. "That's what I thought. Come to the jet, *now*. Crockett will need your help loading an extra passenger."

He took a picture of sleeping beauty with her cell.

CHAPTER 22

I was so busy trying to get a hold of Saki, I missed eight calls from James. A lump developed in my throat as I answered his ninth call. "I can't find my sister." I sobbed.

He hesitated before he spoke. "Where are you? You need to come home."

"I am pulling up right no ..." My stomach tied in knots at the sight of my front door smashed in. "Oh God, oh God, please don't let her be in there." I threw the car in Park, grabbed my gun, and dashed out.

James stood by his GMC truck and took cover with his Glock 27 held at his side. His eyes trained on my house. "Are you armed?"

"Always," I replied.

Without speaking, we walked up tactically.

I covered the windows, James the front.

Since I knew every inch of my residence, I was first man. We cleared my 2000 square foot home with the same two-person entry we'd used a hundred times. Clearing all the hard corners and fatal funnels.

"All clear." We spoke in unison.

As we re-entered the living room, I was no longer in agent mode. I surveyed my house that looked like a tossed Caesar salad. James and I were no strangers to this technique and had pitched a few ourselves over the years.

A red-hot molten fury ascended on me. I blew a fuck fuse. I screamed and unleashed every pent-up, profane word that came to mind. James's big brown eyes widened, and he pinched his lips. Normally, I made it a point to keep my composure and not curse as an example for Saki, who swore like a sailor.

As James picked up my overturned ottoman, we spotted it at the same time. By my banged up safe, was a breaching tool, a battering ram deployed by law enforcement officers.

"We know what he used to break in your door." James removed a pair of black gloves from his back pocket. "And your safe. I'll call dispatch and get the locals out here. CSI will dust it for prints, but I'm sure they won't find any." He inspected the ram. "He most likely wore gloves." James spoke matter-of-factly, as if he were at any old crime scene.

But we weren't. We were in my home. The home Bradley and I bought less than five years ago. My safe harbor. Only now a house of horrors.

James stood with his hand on his hip and gave me a blank stare, glanced away, and looked back, his brow furrowed. "What kind of cop would do this to one of his own?" He pulled his buzzing cell from his pocket. "Hey, I forgot to ask, have you heard from your sister? You don't think, he—"

James stared at the text message. "Um ... Rose, the dude that rented the SUV is a guy by the name of Max Ryan, age thirty-four. No known address. There's a block on it. He's an art dealer from Miami Beach." James stopped reading and gave me a slow stare. "Why would someone in Florida have a beef with you or Saki?"

CHAPTER 23

*F*lorida! My stomach churned, and I felt flushed. I stumbled to the kitchen, opened the freezer, and drew a deep breath. *This can't be happening.* I shut my eyes.

"Rose! Did you hear me?" James slammed the freezer door, stood in front of me. "What connections do you have to Florida?"

"Nothing," I snapped and moved away. I couldn't lie to his face.

"Look at me! I call bullshit. I can't help if you don't talk to me." He raised his voice as he followed me around the kitchen.

"It's long and complicated." I plopped down on the barstool with my head in my hand.

"Make it simple and give me the Reader's Digest version." He crossed his arms and tapped his feet.

"AP, I don't have time to get into it. I've got to find Saki! She's my priority right now." I gave him a pleading look.

Whether it was my expression or using our old Austin Powers nickname, but he softened his interrogation. "Love, what is going on?" He sounded less a cop and more my friend.

My cell chirped. My heart fluttered at Saki's personal text tone. "It's her." My hands fumbled as I pulled my phone out of my pocket. "Something is downloading ... I'll bet she had car prob ..." I stared at the phone in disbelief. My world crashed. A picture. Saki. Hands tied, asleep—*please, God, let her be asleep only*—lying in the back seat of a car. The phone slipped from my grasp.

James caught it. "Oh my God!"

I snatched it back and dialed. It went to voice mail. "I'm going to kill that *mother fucker*." The evil intent in my voice startled both of us as we stared at one another with wide eyes.

I jumped off the stool and immediately felt nauseated. The room spun and closed in on me. James's lips were moving, but I couldn't hear him. My vision telescoped and everything went black.

CHAPTER 24

I came to on the sofa with a wet, cool washcloth on my forehead. James sat at my feet, speaking softly into his phone.

The entire morning was a nightmare, and I was ready to wake up to a reality with Saki safe, down the hallway. Only I was awake and living the nightmare. I started to sit, but James eased me back with one hand. The other disconnected his call.

"How the hell are you going to kill him if you can't remain vertical?" He shot me a sideways glance.

I flung the cloth on the coffee table and sat upright as he handed me a cup of hot peppermint tea with honey. "I'm fine now, thanks." I took a sip. "Who was that?"

"Yeah, you're *fine*! Not that you need to hear

shittier news, but they found Saki's car. It's in the ravine off Maple Street. This Max guy and whoever his accomplice is, wanted it out of sight." James was in full-blown FBI Special Agent Powers mode.

He stood. "CSI will be here in half an hour to dust for prints. I suggest you get dressed. You need to pack a few things. You can't stay here. We'll set up a trace on Saki's phone. I know it's the local's jurisdiction, for now. Unless he takes her across state lines, then we'll ..."

This can't be happening to us. She did nothing wrong. It's me he's after ...

"... and who the fuck authorized the removal of your security detail? Wait until I get my hands on ..." He paced and rambled.

It's all my fault. I stared at him. *I have to do this solo.*

"... you understand, Rose?"

"Okay." I replied, not listening to most of his conversation. "I'll wait for CSI to finish." I faked a grin. "And meet you at the office." For the first time in six years, I lied straight-faced to my friend and partner. I ignored the tightness in my throat at that thought.

James hugged me and told me he wouldn't stop until we found Saki.

As I watched him walk out the door, an empty pit opened in my gut. *This is probably the last time I'll see you, James. I am so sorry.*

An incoming attachment from an unknown number interrupted my goodbye thoughts. It was a picture of Saki restrained in an airplane. Still asleep—drugged? "You're messing with the wrong person!" I said and phoned right back. But he didn't answer.

I texted: *You harm my sister, and you are dead, asshole! What do you want?*

CHAPTER 25

Max watched Saki's eyelids flicker as her head bobbled. Good. She was coming around. Time to ask her some questions.

"Ketamine is my favorite drug. It is quick acting, with less respiratory sedation. You might hallucinate and see double, but don't worry ... it's not permanent," Max said in a low, condescending manner. He stood at the galley, mixing his own martini. His last flight attendant quit without notice when they'd landed in California the other day. He shook the gin and vermouth, then poured it into a glass, added two olives.

Max sipped his drink as he made his way to the couch across from Saki. He leaned over and brushed her messy blonde waves away from her face and stared. "It's a shame to hide such beauty."

She jerked her head and her eyes flew open. "Wha' hap ... where am I?" Her words were breathy and inaudible. Saki wiggled but a shoulder seatbelt held her in place. Her wrists were bound together with plastic ties in front of her. Her ankles were free. "What the fck?" She slurred and frowned, gazing down at her hands.

"Tsk, tsk. You and your sister have such foul mouths." He read the last text from Rose. "If you don't behave, I'll have to give you more sleeping juice."

Saki scanned the jet interior, the plush seats, the galley, the door to his bedroom. He could see comprehension and lucidity return to her mind.

"And you can't go anywhere. We're cruising at an altitude of 41,000 feet."

"Who'r you? Where we goin?" She shook her head.

"You questioning me? No, no, that's not how this works, pretty girl."

"How what works and who the hell are you?" Saki snarled as her speech returned.

Max crossed his leg and swirled his olive. "I don't look familiar to you?"

Saki observed him through narrow eyes. "Other than the pizza guy."

"I'm not surprised. I was eleven, and you were ... two? Twenty-three years flies in the blink of an eye."

"So, why the fuck did you kidnap me? To

rehash old times?" She glared at him.

"No, my dear. I'd prefer to forget them. But your sister has something that belonged to my father and I want it back."

"What do I have to do with it?"

"You have everything to do with it." He whispered and enunciated every word.

"Why should I believe you? You could be some random sick fuck who preys on women." Saki thrust her chin forward.

"Trust me, I don't need to kidnap women to get what I want from them. And let's just say our fathers were business partners and best friends many years ago, before you were even born. Until yours tore mine away."

"Bullshit. My father never did such a thing. He died overseas in combat. He was a hero," she screamed.

"So, that's the lie they fed you? Ha, ha. I'm going to have fun with you. No, princess, your father died in prison."

"You're a lying, crazy son-of-a-bitch!" Saki lunged, but her restraints jerked her back.

"Don't call me that!" Max glared.

"What? Crazy or son-of-a-bitch?"

He bolted up, baring his teeth. "*Both*." He slapped her. Blood splattered against the window. "My mother was not a *whore*. She was an angel."

Saki licked her lip as blood dripped in her mouth. "Jeez, I've taught mixed martial arts to eight-year-old girls who hit me harder. Is that all you got ... mamma's boy?!"

Max took a deep breath and snapped the

rubber band on his wrist. He slipped back to the galley and retrieved the loaded syringe from the top drawer.

This time Saki saw it coming. She shrank back in the seat, but had nowhere to go.

He watched her nod off and picked up his cell phone.

Max: *Give me the Falcon!*

Rose: *Falcon?? What are u talking about?*

Max: *Don't play games ... Rose Reagan! I know who you are.*

CHAPTER 26

"**R**ose Reagan?!" I dropped the phone and plopped onto Bradley's leather La-Z-Boy recliner. "This couldn't be, she ... she ceased to exist. Who is this guy? And the Falcon?!" I quaked.

I was seven the last time I heard her name, and my world had turned upside down. My father left and Mother was a wreck. His parting words molded me. Some would ask who'd put that burden on a child. I never gave it a second thought and did what I was told.

After the feds moved us around safe houses, we relocated across the country. My mom insisted on returning to her birth name. So, at eight, Rose O'Brien was born, and never looked back, until today. My mother warned me if anyone came searching for the Reagans, trouble was close.

As I slumped in the chair praying for guidance, I stared at the powder where the CSI team had dusted for latent fingerprints. It hit me like a bolt of lightning. The answer was in the gun safe. I rushed over and tossed the contents on the dining room table. And found it stuck between pictures of our parents and my passport. An envelope with Rosie drawn in cursive. Hours before her death, my mother handed it to me. But in my grief, I forgot, or perhaps was in denial.

I paced a hole in the carpet as my trembling hands held Mom's final written words. Just as I worked up the courage to unseal it, a Master Lock key fell out. "What the heck?" I picked it up and rolled it around in my fingers as I read the letter.

My mouth dropped open.

... the Falcon is in a storage unit, climate-controlled, in Key West—blah, blah— paid for a year. The unit has two locks. Here is one key, the other is in Grandma Rosie May O'Brien's mausoleum in the Key West City Cemetery. I am sorry. It was the safest place.

She gave me the number of a trusted friend, Kirk Tubberious, Tubbs for short. He piloted his own plane and would do anything for the family, no questions asked.

"My kind of guy." I picked up my phone and dialed. "Hello, Tubbs?"

CHAPTER 27

Finally, a piece of good luck. Tubbs had flown into California two days ago from Miami Beach. His niece had an interview for a residency position at U.C. Davis. Coincidentally, he'd filed a flight plan to Key West for this afternoon.

Just like Mom said, Tubbs asked no questions and refused payment. He said he was an old family friend who owed Teddy a favor. Given my father's criminal history, I did not want to know the extent of their *favors*.

Don't ask a question, you don't want the answer to, my dad used to say.

After our fifteen-minute conversation, I finished packing a few essentials, including my mini arsenal of handguns and ammo. I penned a letter to James telling him sorry and goodbye and wrote another of resignation. Once my department discovered I'd lied, I'd be fired anyway. I made a final request to James, asking him to turn my letter over to my supervisor. I left both notes on the dining room table along with my keys, badge, and cell phone.

As I reached the front door, I turned around and wiped the tear that fell. The journey ahead was a one-way trip.

It didn't matter. This haven was void of my loved ones who had made it a home.

CHAPTER 28

"**W**here the hell is she?" James bellowed in the car as he called Rose for the tenth time. "Something's wrong." As soon as he disconnected, it buzzed again. Titianos read the screen. Finally. "What did you find out for me?" he snapped.

"Good morning to you too, Agent Powers."

"Tony, I'm sorry, man. I don't have time for small talk."

Tony Leroy Titianos, James's counterpart in Miami, was from New York but sounded more like a member of the mafia than an FBI Agent. James had worked with Tony on a few cases before and had asked him to run a local record's check on Maxwell Ryan out of Miami Beach.

"Ryan is clean. He probably whistles when he walks. Not even as much as a speeding ticket. He's a bigwig art dealer in Miami Beach. He's not ya man."

"He was just here and rented a couple vehicles," James barked.

"Hey man, don't shoot the messenger. I am on ya side."

James drew a deep and deliberate breath and exhaled. "Sorry, Tony, but I have reason to believe Max kidnapped my partner's sister. I lost contact with her ... so, you see the urgency here?" He spoke through gritted teeth.

"Okay, okay, I got it. Send me the work up on the case, including ya partner's info. I'll do more checking and get back to ya."

"Thanks, man, I appreciate it."

James took a sharp turn into the driveway and jumped out of the car. He used his key to enter Rose's home. An eerie, vacant feeling fell over him.

He strode to the garage door, flung it open. Her Highlander was there. He groaned as he drew his gun.

"Rose, Rose, are you in here?" He conducted a one-person search, calling and opening the door to every room. "Shit, she packed in a hurry," James mumbled as he re-holstered his weapon.

He returned to the front room and saw an envelope sitting on the table. As he opened it, the contents dropped out. He slumped on the chair as he read the note. "What kind of trouble are you in?"

He ran a hand over his face. "Well, at least I know she wasn't kidnapped too … but then wh…" His phone buzzed and he peeked at the caller ID. "Daisy, I need good news."

"Agent Powers. Daisy here, sir." A fast-talking intel analyst chirped.

"Yes, I can see that, please don't call me sir. I work for a living. Whatcha got for me?"

Daisy continued as if she were a hamster on a wheel. "Maxwell Ryan is not his birth name. He changed it. He also has a juvie record, but a Miami federal judge sealed it. I'll have to do more digging. I have friends out there who owe me. Ryan is also loaded, he has houses all over the world, at least two in Florida. One in South Beach, and the other in Key West. He probably has a matching watch for every day of the week. Any luck on Agent O'Brien?"

"Nope, she went off the grid."

"Do you want me to ping her phone?"

"She dumped it, most likely bought a burner." He let out a poof of air. "Text me Max's addresses and the rest of the information, including his photo. Can you also run an airline passenger manifesto?"

James could hear her nails hitting the keyboard at lightning speed. "One step ahead of you. I'm sending you Ryan's info right … now. I'm checking the passenger manifestos as we speak. Just give me two."

"Thanks, Daisy. And lay off the coffee. It'll give you a heart attack."

"But I don't drink cof—"

James ended the call. "I love my intel geeks."

He went through the house one more time looking for clues. He stood by the empty safe when his phone buzzed with an incoming text.

Daisy: *Negative on any flight manifesto. She closed her bank accounts a few hrs. ago. There were two flight plans filed from Auburn to Key West. One by Max, early this morning and the other by one Kirk Tubberious, it's taking off now.*

He sighed. "You closed your bank accounts and chartered a private plane, you resourceful little brat."

James tapped out a reply as he hurried out of the house.

Thnx D. Have the boss call me. I need his blessing to head out. Also, run a background on Tubberious.

Daisy: *On it. Boss said all good. No flights to the Keys, but you R on the red eye to Miami, nothing sooner, sorry. Arrive 8:00 AM. Reserved you a vehicle and booked you into the Palm Island Hotel in Key West. We assume that is where you're headed ;-) Here is your boarding pass.*

He called his counterpart. "Hey, Tony, it's Powers again." James told him the whole story. After all, if he couldn't trust another FBI agent, who could he trust?

CHAPTER 29

Tubbs was taller than I'd pictured. A lean man in his early sixties, with shiny black hair, wearing a straw hat with aviator sunglasses perched on top. He could've stepped out of a *Tommy Bahama* catalogue in his bright floral silk shirt, tan cargo shorts, and dockers with no socks.

"Good afternoon. You must be Rose." He greeted me with a Greek accent and a warm hug. Tubbs took my bags from the rolling cart. "Oh, a bit heavy." He winked. As he loaded them on his Cessna Citation CJ4, we chatted about the weather and he advised me we'd make it to the Keys without stopping. We'd covered the logistics of the trip during our earlier conversation.

As I made my way up the short steps to

board the plane, a familiar voice called out in the distance. Butterflies fluttered in my heart. I turned around, hoping it wasn't a mirage and Saki was truly running across the tarmac. As the woman drew closer, reality slapped my face.

She panted as she approached. "*Holy moly*." She wiped the sweat from her forehead. "Sorry I'm late, Uncle T." She bounced up the steps and removed her backpack. "Traffic was horrible, and the Uber driver got lost."

As she rambled, she twisted her long, wavy strawberry blonde hair. "Hi, I am Kaylee Tubberious ... have we met?" She tilted her head.

I studied her then blinked when she flushed under my long gaze and looked away. "Um ... no. We haven't. I'm Rose." We shook hands, and an image of my dad flashed in my brain. I cleared my throat and dismissed it to the heat and lack of sleep, not to mention the gaping hole in my shoulder.

"Whoa, you're bleeding, let me fix this." She grabbed my free hand and led me to the back of the plane.

"I'm ... fine?" I shrugged and gave Tubbs a quizzical look.

A smile crinkled the corner of his eyes, and he laughed. "She is persistent. Don't worry, she is top of her class, you're in excellent hands." He spoke with a puffed chest. "My niece has had practice." He removed his hat and pointed to a faint scar. "She knows I won't go to the hospital." Tubbs handed Kaylee a black and orange EMS bag from the rear compartment. "Never leaves home without it."

I was too exhausted to fight and watched her work, hands and manner calm and competent. I knew we'd never met ... yet I couldn't shake the feeling our paths had crossed.

CHAPTER 30

During the five-hour flight to the Keys, Kaylee told me her life story. She was born and raised in Miami Beach. Her mother lived in Miami, and her father was not in the picture. It was something we had in common, absent fathers. Kaylee was in medical school at the University of Florida and one semester from graduating.

I shared with her that Saki and I grew up in San Diego and both graduated from U.C. San Diego. I kept the intimate details of my life close to the vest. *Trust no one*, was my motto. It was a hazard of my job, and to a certain extent my childhood. With Kaylee, I had a burning desire to confess my deepest, darkest secrets. But I didn't.

When we landed in Key West, it was five in

the evening, East Coast time. Kaylee and I said our goodbyes and exchanged phone numbers. She told me she was on summer break, staying with her boyfriend, and only a call away.

Tubbs rented a car for me under his name. His paternal instinct to take care of me felt over the top. I grew up without a father and didn't need one now. But I was also raised to be gracious. So, I thanked him and left cash in the cockpit when he wasn't looking. He may have owed Teddy, not me.

As I exited the terminal, the heavy, sticky humidity nearly knocked me off my feet, and I had the urge to shower again. The second I jumped in the maroon Chevy Malibu, I blasted the AC and lifted my shirt over the vents.

Just then I received my first text on my burner phone. Only Max and Kaylee had my new number, so I knew it was from him. I'd programed a special contact name for him.

Ass Hole: *Welcome to Key West, Ms. Reagan. You now have twenty-four hours to get me the Falcon.*

An empty pit opened in my stomach. *How did he know I was here?*

I shot back a reply.

I want proof of life.

CHAPTER 31

As the old adage says, *Desperate times call for desperate measures*. I hit the rock bottom of desperation as I headed for the Key West City Cemetery. It was at the center of Old Town, just under ten minutes from the airport along scenic US A1A.

I drove up to the main gate on Passover Lane and went to the sexton's office and asked directions to Killian and Rosie O'Brien's family mausoleum. My grandparents died within two days of one other at the ripe ages of 94 and 96. The sexton directed me to my clan's crypt somewhere between 3rd and 4th streets.

I strolled the nineteen-acre park-like cemetery and passed whitewashed, above ground tombs and statues that were both witty and fascinating. I stopped at one epitaph that read, *I told you I was sick*. If I were not on my way to violate the sanctity of my grandparents' final resting spot, I would have read more.

I blended in with other visitors who showed up hoping to take a tour of the quirky, crowded, historic cemetery. I passed the infamous pet deer, Elfina, and found my grandparents on 4th Ave. The O'Brien's crypt contained eight family members, including my maternal grandparents who rested side by side, and six others who migrated from Ireland searching for a better life.

I kept my head on a swivel for passing tourists as I approached the concrete pillars. The second I stepped inside, the stench knocked me off my feet. While there was no seepage from the bodies, the humidity caused unsavory smells. I stretched my shirt over my face and held my breath, as if it would block out the odor. Early in my career I learned Vick's VapoRub under the nose would do the trick in cases of an olfactory nightmare, such as this. *Note to self, buy later*.

I spied Grandma and Grandpa, front and center, and sprung out, leaving the door ajar for my midnight return. The second I hit fresh air, I coughed so loud it could have raised the dead. As I bent over trying to catch my breath, a couple passed and asked if I were okay. I gave them a thumbs up, and they kept on going.

On the way back to the rental car, I noticed ominous billowing cotton-wool clouds looming on the horizon.

CHAPTER 32

It was five-thirty and still hotter than a firefly's ass as I drove around Key West looking for hotels that didn't require ID. I pulled up to one on notorious Duval Street, but a prima donna front desk clerk shot me a nasty look and rejected me. Sure, I smelled foul and was saturated in sweat, but I had money, a lot of it.

After she scanned me with a scowl, she pointed me to a back-alley, filthy, rat trap cash only, with hourly rates. The Palm Breeze. It was anything but a breeze and catered to hookers and fugitives. But it was the only available motel where I could hide under the radar.

I checked in, showered, and wolfed a burger, fries, and a coke. While fast food was not on my usual menu, I had no appetite and needed it for sustenance. It also soaked up the expired Vicodin I had from dental surgery a year ago. While drugs were not my thing, it had only been five days since the shooting and pain coursed through my body.

As I chomped down a Whopper, it brought back memories of my college days when I partied too much and the only thing that helped was grease. I'd give my right arm to be back there. Instead, I was holed up in a shitty hotel, hiding from a mad man and popping old pills.

After a half hour the medication kicked in, so I yanked off the top blanket and evicted any visible resident bed bugs. The fresh bleach tingled my nose. *At least the hotel washed their sheets,* I reasoned as I faded to the rain drops pattering against the window and fell into a long nap.

CHAPTER 33

Saki blinked as Max's phone lit up with an incoming call. He'd just dragged her into this large, dank room and taken off her blindfold. He answered the call on speaker for some reason. Wanting her to hear how he had minions doing his bidding? "What is it?"

"Hey, Boss, we got a problem."

"What now?" Max roared.

"An FBI agent in California inquired about your guest. He's on a red-eye flight and should arrive tomorrow morning."

"Titos, do I have to tell you how to do your job? Just deal with it." Max ended the call. He shoved Saki away and she stumbled. He slipped out the door and slammed it. He must have an intercom because she heard his voice still. "Pound and scream all you want, no one can hear you, Saki." He mocked. "I modified this place for my ... special guests." She made a rude gesture toward the dark pane of glass. "And flipping me off won't help your cause either."

"Special guests? You sick fuck." She screamed and pounded her fists on the one-way window. "Get in here, you fucking coward, and face me like a man." She continued ranting.

Twenty minutes later, sweat saturated her clothes after Saki's investigation of the dimly lit thirty by forty foot cell. She discovered gray soundproof panels on three sides, covered by a black curtain. The fourth wall was one-way mirrored glass. There were no visible windows or doors. The only amenities were a tattered wooden chair and an old army cot.

Saki was not a quitter, but her hope of escaping looked futile as the mugginess overwhelmed her. She attempted to draw a deep breath, but her legs gave out and she found herself on the clammy concrete floor.

As Saki pondered her fate, a dank, musty smell hung in the air. Suddenly, she spotted an object in the far corner. As she drew closer, she gasped, "Oh my *God*! This is a torture chamber." The fine hairs on Saki's body stood on end as she stared at the blood-stained drain. Max had no intention of releasing her.

A red heaping volcano erupted in her gut.

CHAPTER 34

Gunshots rang out. I jerked awake and grabbed my compact Glock 40 from the nightstand. In the darkness, I held my breath for an eternity. A flashback to the shooting was only the sound of the skies unleashing the caged kraken. It boomed and snapped again and sent shock waves of pain through my body.

It took a second for me to return to the reality of my lumpy bed in a shit-bag motel. I blinked a few times to shake the Vicodin-induced fog from my brain and squinted out the window. Night had fallen fast.

As I flipped on the light, I rolled over and peeked at the clock. "Crap! Eleven forty-five, I'm late." I slithered out of bed, put my gun back down, and slipped into my shoes before my feet hit the sticky carpet then shuffled to the bathroom. I'd slept in my street clothes and stayed ready.

My last pain pill awaited me, so I gulped it with warm Pepsi. Standing in front of the cracked mirror, a set of sad, vacant, aged blue eyes stared back. Not the aging that comes with fine wine or cheese, but the cheap kind, two-buck Chuck and generic cheddar.

As I peered around the sleazy suite, I realized my world was a colossal shit show. I was on a one-woman crusade to save my sister from a psycho. *How much worse could it get?*

CHAPTER 35

I should know better than to ask that question. A loud thumping interrupted my pity party "Yeah, who is it?" I grumbled.

"Manager," said a muffled voice.

I glanced at the clock, and it was midnight. *I don't think so.* I frowned. I backed up to retrieve my pistol from the nightstand, but I was too slow.

He took up the entire doorway, a tall, thick-bodied battering-ram of a man. I didn't have time to react and sidestepped left before he ran straight into the lamp, knocking it on the floor. The room went dark and my Glock was out of reach.

"Who the fuck are you?" I screamed as I smashed the lamp over his skull.

"Ahh, bitch!" He shook his head as if he were

shaking off droplets of water. His right punch grazed my wounded shoulder. I landed on the ground.

"*Mother fucker*!" I refused to surrender to the pain and bolted up like a jack rabbit. We stood face to chest as he towered over my five-foot eight broken frame. Out of instinct, I moved into a bladed self-defense stance with my right leg back. He followed suit. Since I was weaponless, this would not be a fair fight.

I pulled my left leg up and to the side and snapped it as fast as I could. I delivered the fiercest Roundhouse kick of my life. I hit him so deep in the groin, Google Earth would not have been able to find his nuts.

He doubled over. "Yo ... you bitch!" I took advantage of his low position and swung at his face with an open palm heel strike. I needed to leave my mark. He slumped to his knees.

I retrieved my gun from the floor where it had fallen and drew down on him, flipping on the dim overhead light. "Let me see your hands, *asshole*! Who the hell are you? Why are you here?"

My assailant's dingy brown hair was wet with humidity, and his hazel eyes had red spider veins running through them. As he hunched over and grabbed his crotch, a neck badge fell from behind his shirt.

"Seriously! You're a cop?" I drew a heavy breath. "Yo ... you were the one who sacked my house. I could pop your ass right now and get away with it."

"Hey, take it easy, Rose." He waved a hand

of surrender as he hunched over. "I'm here to deliver a message. Max said *no cops*. You brought this on yourself."

"I didn't bring any cops. I came alone."

He lowered his hands.

"You reach for it, I shoot."

"If I wanted to kill ya, I would have shot ya with that stupid kid."

"Jessie? That was you! He sent you to kidnap me, so why kill—"

"The kid grew a conscience and was gonna confess."

I glared at him as the blood drained from my body. "To what?" I waved my Glock. I needed to hear it.

"Why do ya think there were no skid marks?" He inched closer to the door.

The room grew smaller and hotter. "You hired Jessie to cut Brad's brakes ... why ...?" I fumed with my remaining breath.

"How do you think we found you?" he fired back.

As I ranted, a warm, sticky sensation trickled down my left arm. I saw a bright red stream and stumbled backward in the bathroom, hitting my forehead against the sink.

The coward bolted as I crawled to my cell phone. The numbers were blurry as blood clouded my eyes. "Help ... Palm Breeze ... 22 ..."

I'd hit rock bottom. I thought.

CHAPTER 36

"**L**ooks like I arrived in time." I blinked and Kaylee came into focus. She stood over me with a terrified expression.

"Wha ... what time is it?" I mumbled.

"Quarter to one."

I dropped back as quick as I'd sat up.

"Easy, Wonder Woman. You're not going anywhere." She helped me off the bathroom floor and onto the bed. It relieved me she didn't see my gun that had slid under a towel during the scuffle.

"I have to go, fix me up ... I'll pay you whatever you want."

"You split your stitches wide open, and you have a laceration to your head."

"Kaylee, you don't understand. I don't care

... never mind, please hurry!"

"Rose, I know we just met ..." She scanned my room. "But, you're in real trouble. Let me help you. I'll call my unc—"

"I have to do this alone ... I'm fine. I got dizzy and fell and broke the lamp," I said with a half-hearted smile I hoped was reassuring.

She slid on white surgical gloves and examined my wound, disregarding my lie. "You need stitches. I have to take you to a hospital."

"*No*, no, hospitals. I know you can do this. You did it for your uncle. Please!"

"Rose, this is serious. You have major blood loss, not to mention I could get into a lot of trouble."

"I swear on my sister's life." I grabbed her shirt. "I won't tell a soul." Who would believe me? I was pleading for my life in a bed bug-ridden motel and I was on my way to desecrate my families' crypt to save my sister. That's one for the story books.

Now this was rock bottom.

Kaylee puffed her cheeks and exhaled. "Okay," she said without emotion. She produced a wad of gauze. "Put this in your mouth and bite hard." I looked at her as if she'd lost her mind. "Trust me, do it. This is going to hurt like the devil."

She was right. The dam burst as I let out a muffled scream.

"Rose, I am so sorry." She stared at me with Labrador eyes.

Forty-five minutes passed, and Kaylee completed her first motel surgery. She resutured my shoulder and stitched my forehead. She glanced around again. "Rose, what really happened?" She shot me a loving and reassuring smile. "You can trust me."

My mouth opened, but words didn't come out. I craved with every inch of my broken soul to unload this beast of burden I had been carrying since childhood, but I couldn't. Not yet.

Instead, I pulled out a couple hundred from my wallet and handed it to her.

"Someday." She gave it back. "Besides, you already paid my uncle." She cast a sideways glance. Kaylee packed up her bag and threw the blood-stained towel and dressing in the trash and approached the broken door.

"I owe you big time," I said. "Oh, and make sure you're not followed."

She nodded and turned. "I wish you believed in me ..." She flicked her wrist. "And whatever this is, you can't do it alone. You need to ask for help. You're not really Wonder Woman, Rose."

As I rolled off the bed, I realized my father used to call me his *little superhero*. I shrugged. Weird.

CHAPTER 37

As daylight inched over the ocean, I made my way to the cemetery. At five a.m., it was somewhere between astronomical and nautical twilight. My unexpected visitor caused me to lose the cover of night. For my sake, I did recon upon my arrival and found the perfect spot to back in my Malibu.

I sprinted into the crypt's alcove and shined my mag light. The second my foot hit the step, I slipped in a couple inches of watery mud accumulated from the early morning storm and dropped the light. Just as I bent to shake it loose from the muck, two figures emerged from 4th Avenue.

"Crap!" I murmured and shut off the light. In the darkness, keys jangled from their belts. As they drew closer, the keys mocked me with every step. *You failed ... you failed.* I shook in disagreement. *Failure is not an option.* I tugged on the concrete door with all my muster and just as they were three mausoleums over, I sucked in my stomach and squeezed inside the vault. The mocking voice stopped.

"How did this get opened?" A heavily Cuban accented male questioned. "Come on, help me close it."

They grunted and swore as they pushed, but it did not budge. "I'm going to grab the shovel, wait here," he said.

"Hell, no! I'm going with you," replied a deep croaky voiced man.

I listened as they jangled away and let out a huge exhale under my shirt. I placed the flashlight inside my sling and illuminated the crypt and found Grandpa and Grandma again, still front and center.

As I poked in the crevices between their vaults, a warm, gooey substance dripped down my fingers. The stench worsened the deeper my fingers slid and seared my nose hairs. It occurred to me the tomb seeped.

"Okay, Rose, this is by far the most disgusting thing you have ever done," I murmured. In my line of work, I had seen my share of dead and decaying bodies, but I never defiled them. As I dug deeper, I felt something hard in the goo. Hoping it was only the key, I plucked away until it broke free, taking a chunk of something with me.

I apologized to my deceased relatives for violating their final resting place and asked

God for forgiveness. Legend had it that the ghost of a mysterious Bahamian woman would terrify anyone disrespectful during their visit to the graveyard. My actions were beyond disrespectful, they were categorically criminal.

A moment of relief fell over me as I put the fluid-drenched key in my pocket and shook off the rest of the goo from my hand onto the ground. I pressed through the cinder block door to discover it half-way closed, no thanks to the groundskeepers.

I pushed as hard as my broken body allowed. Between the 100% humidity and the overwhelming stench, I dry heaved and spit on the floor. In the distance, the jingling returned. My heart stopped.

"Brace yourself, Rose. One, two, three … Shiiit!" I removed my arm from the sling and held it straight to my side, pain surging through my body and perspiration dripping into my stitches. *Adding salt to injury* was not just an idiom, it's the real deal.

As I popped my head out and exhaled, I had an image of *The Shining*. Instead of *Here's Johnny*, it was *Here's Rosie*.

Just then a frightened male screamed. "What are you doing?"

With my adrenaline on octane, I catapulted the rest of my body out of the crypt and bolted past them, not looking back. I jumped in the car, started it, threw it in gear, and pulled away, tires screeching.

CHAPTER 38

James landed at the Miami International airport at nine a.m., rented a car, and made the thirty-five-minute drive to the Miami-Dade FBI building.

"Tony Titianos, please," James said to the short, gray-haired security guard who greeted him. Most of the guards were retired cops, double dipping for an easy gig. The officer checked James's ID, handed him a pass, and directed him upstairs.

"Agent Powers." Tony limped up and offered a firm handshake. Tony missed his calling and should have been a WWE Wrestler. He stood six four and easily weighed two hundred fifty pounds. His face bore the markings of a recent fight.

"Agent Titianos, how are you?" James

scanned his hobbling coworker.

"Ya know, Powers, same shit, different toilet," he said with an upturned lip.

James shot him a confused look.

"Disregard, I guess ya not a fan of the cheesy Segal movies."

"What happened?"

"I was playing football and hey, shit happens," he replied with a laugh. "And my friends call me Titos." Titos leaned in and lowered his voice. "Hey, sorry you came out here for nutin'. I still don't have anything new to report on that Maxwell dude. He is as clean as they come. But, ya know." He winked. "While you are here, I can set ya up with some real nice girls for a night on the town."

James stared at him. A slow, suspicious fury brewed at his counterpart's lack of professionalism. He cocked his chin. "Hm, strange, that's not what my people found," James snapped. "Who did your research?" He raised his voice a notch and planted his fists on his hips.

"Chill, Powers." Titos motioned with his hands as if slowing traffic. He looked around the room as everyone stopped what they were doing and stared. He shot James a look and nodded to his left. "Come in here, we got more privacy."

James followed him to a closet sized office. He stood with his arms crossed as he glared across the desk at Titos.

"Sit, James, you're making me nervous."

"No, thanks. They say sitting is worse for you

than smoking."

"We have little time, Titos. Every second counts on these kidnapping cases."

"Yeah, yeah. So, watcha got on Max?"

James gazed at Titos, considered.

"Come on, Powers. How can I help you out, if you ain't gonna be straight wit me?"

James sighed, dropped into the chair. "Max changed his name when he was a juvenile, but one of your Miami judges sealed it. My intel geeks are still working on his identity."

"Copy that, but on the phone you told me your agent friend is here looking for Saki. Who this Max guy allegedly kidnapped?"

"Not allegedly, he did. And yes, I believe she is in Key West. I'm headed there now."

Titos wiped the sweat from his brow and loosened his tie. "So, uh, are you in contact with Rose?"

"No. She dumped her cell and disappeared. I was hoping for assistance from locals in the Keys and you guys."

"I'll talk to the boss. But ya need to know he don't play nice with West Coast fibbies. He can be a real asshole sometimes." Titos leaned back in his chair.

"Your bureau chief Kevin O'Malley? An asshole? He's good people."

"Nah, someone new. O'Malley got promoted again." Titos rolled his eyes. "Bigwig O'Malley heads up a specialized bullshit stolen art team. Kevin is based out of DC but has an office next door. He's on a special assignment in the field today." Titos stood. "Hey, why don't you check into your hotel. I'll grab some locals, and we'll get eyes on Max's place. Let's meet up at Key West PD this afternoon."

On his way downstairs, James called and left O'Malley a voice message. They'd worked together years ago. He'd trust O'Malley's take on Titos.

As James exited the Federal Building, he peered up and spotted Titos at his window, talking on his cell. He raised his hand in farewell at James.

The hair on James's neck rose. "I didn't tell him Saki's name."

CHAPTER 39

"That agent is here, and he knows everything." Titos pulled the phone away from his ear as Max shouted threats.

Titos cursed his involvement with Max, but he'd been drowning in the shallow end of the debt pool when a friend introduced them. Titos had two ex-wives who drained his bank account and a betting problem. He'd reluctantly agreed to do a couple of jobs for Max in exchange for paying off his bookie. Two led to three then another and another. The money was better than what the feds paid him. Titos tried to get out, but Max threatened to tell the FBI about his illegal projects. Now, Max owned Titos.

Finally, Titos shouted, "Calm down, I'll deal

with him."

Max threw his cell and stormed into the room where Saki had fallen asleep. "*Get up.*" He kicked her cot.

Saki jolted awake. "What the ..." She was tired and hungry, but no longer under the influence of Ketamine. She jumped to her feet and stood nose to nose with Max and narrowed her eyes. "If you treat me like a dog one more time, you will be a sorry mother fucker!" Saki growled through gritted teeth.

Ah. She was ready for a fight. Max grabbed her by the neck and pulled her hair. His one-of-a-kind cologne that had once sent her into a tizzy, now seemed to sicken her. She drew back with a wrinkled nose, then punched his jaw. He twisted her arm and put her in a choke hold.

"You see, you're not the only one who's had training," he whispered in her ear. "I could snap your pretty neck in a second. For now, I'll let you go." He released his grip, threw her across the room onto the cot.

Max rubbed his face. "I figured you'd grow up to be feisty."

She squinted and studied him.

"Ah, finally, speechless." Max pulled up the wooden chair and told her the rest of the dirty little secrets Rose hid from her.

Saki's brow furrowed. "No, no. My sister would never keep that from me ... unless she had good reas ..." She peered at the floor. "Nuh-uh, why should I believe someone as fucked up as you? Why should I believe someone who has a soundproof chamber in his house where he tortures and murders people!" She bolted up from the cot.

"Saki, I may be many things, but I am not a liar." Max stood and headed toward the hidden door.

"Okay, answer me something." She asked in a monotone. "Are you going to kill me?"

He turned back to her. "Yes, but not right now." He stepped to the door.

CHAPTER 40

The sun rose above the horizon while I burned rubber. I called Kaylee en route to the storage unit and asked her to check me into a less cockroach-infested hotel without hourly rates. She obliged and said we needed to talk. I shrugged her off. That seemed a strange request since we just met.

It was seven a.m. by the time I arrived at the You-Store on Shell Street. The building was set in an obscure location behind an alley, with twenty-four-hour surveillance.

A wave of sadness fell upon me as I stood at the threshold. The thought of Max owning the last piece of valuable artwork belonging to my parents sickened and enraged me. I put my emotions aside and approached the only thing standing between me and Saki.

According to Mom's letter, the Falcon was located in the corner of a seventy-five square foot unit. I fumbled with both locks, but they finally yielded to the two keys. I pushed the door open, then shone my phone's flashlight around the dark interior. Boxes and furniture made an obstacle course to the far corner, but I finally made it.

The Falcon sat in a shipping container, wrapped in moving blankets, surrounded by bubble wrap, and fortified with packaging tape. I removed the painting, carried it out, and secured it in the backseat of the car as if it were an infant.

As I made my way to the Palm Island Hotel, I drove in circles to make sure no one followed. Before I exited, I sat in my Chevy for ten minutes and scanned the parking lot for anyone suspicious. Once inside, I barricaded the door with the dresser. Yeah, I know. My paranoia bordered on pathological. But the memory of the cop who busted in the door of my last room and nearly killed me, urged the paranoia to take control.

After I showered the crypt stench off, I gawked at the package. I'd never touched, let alone laid eyes on, anything worth five million dollars, except in galleries. It took me fifteen minutes to peel off the protective layers.

I stepped back, anguish tightening my chest. "This can't be the Falcon. This has got to be a joke." A 24 x 30 framed acrylic painting of Key West taunted me. It belonged in a hotel lobby, not in someone's art collection. I grabbed my phone and opened the web browser.

The Falcon is the third and final painting in the *Birds of Prey Trilogy*. A French artist by the name of Homer Van Titan painted them in 1925. The Trilogy was collectively worth ten million dollars. But the Falcon had a sole value of five million.

I dropped to the floor and sobbed. My world crashed. I had nothing to offer Max. The Falcon was a hoax.

CHAPTER 41

J ames peered out his upstairs hotel window and eyed the thunderhead clouds rolling over the horizon while he spoke on the phone to his trusted friend, Special Agent in Charge Kevin O'Malley. They were in the same academy, but Kevin soared through the ranks of the FBI, while James relished being a field agent.

"Mm hmm ... so, Maxwell Ryan is Samuel Alexander, and he did juvie time?"

"Yep. He changed his name right after they released him from the hall, around age seventeen," O'Malley answered.

"What was his offense?"

"Involuntary manslaughter. He was sixteen. But, due to special circumstances, Max served less than a year in Miami-Dade juvie lockup."

"Who was the vic?" James sat at the desk, put his cell phone on speaker, ready to jot down the information.

"Hmm ..." James could hear papers shuffling. "They redacted that info. Those morons gave me a freakin' redacted report, son of a bitch! I'll order another."

"Probably not important. What else you got?"

"Max is in the family business. The Alexanders have been around for generations. His father, Maxwell Alexander, got them into art. He took a huge loan from a Columbian cartel and hooked up with a partner, Theodore Reagan. They became big time art dealers in Southern Florida. They owned a series of thriving galleries called M.T. Art. That is until they ran a multi-million-dollar scam."

"How the hell do you scam art?" James shot a quizzical look at his phone.

"I always say that greed is the enemy of honest people. And those two would have been poster children for greed. They owned galleries across the states of Florida and New York and managed the acquisition and sale of art. It was legit at first.

"M.T. Art oversold the value of paintings. They'd offer one person the opportunity to buy a share of a work, claiming they could resell it for a quick profit. Then they'd give three other buyers the same deal. Most times they didn't have ownership or control. Maxwell and Theodore collected one hundred percent of the paintings' value."

"Shit, I'm in the wrong business. How did you get so art savvy?"

"I majored in Art History in college. To impress a girl, of course. Then I got hooked. Now I'm spearheading the team. Life is crazy."

"So, how did these guys get caught?"

"By the time the FBI got wind of their activities, they had just filed for bankruptcy. But during this entire ordeal, Theodore wanted out. An argument ensued, and Theodore shot Maxwell. It was ruled an accident. When the feds arrested Theodore, he rolled over on a few high-ranking members of the cartel that loaned Max his startup money. In exchange for Teddy's testimony, they placed his family in witness protection and sent him to an undisclosed federal pen."

"Whoa! What info do you have on the family?"

"Not much. He had a wife and two girls, ages seven and two. All three were given new identities and relocated. Their records sealed."

"It all starts to make sense," James mumbled.

"Huh?"

"I have a hunch my partner and her sister are those girls." James ran his hands through his hair.

"If you're correct, this guy Max wants revenge."

"Yeah, we don't have much time left. Max has two Florida residences that we know of, one in Miami and the other in Key West. We'll hit 'em simultaneously. He can be holding Saki anywhere."

"Dude, I know. This is one of my biggest cases. I've been working on it for the past year. But all my leads went cold, and witnesses came up missing. Max owns people in prominent places. And we need proof he has Saki, not just your hunch. I'll have my guys sit on both locations—"

"*Not* Titos, I don't trust him."

"Don't worry, I won't. We haven't been able to catch Max because we suspected he had a dirty cop on his payroll. Until today, I never dreamed he was one of our own. I want that asshole!"

"You and me both." James picked up his phone.

"Okay, brother, I'm headed your way, but watch your back. I may not be the only one at your door."

They disconnected and James stood.

Saki, hang in there. We're coming.

CHAPTER 42

I gazed at the fraud sitting in front of me. Through my tear-soaked eyes, a bright beam of light shone through the curtain and blinded me. Just as I put my hand up to block the glare, I noticed a tear in the lower left corner of this magnificent piece of crap.

"No freaking way." I let out an exhilarated squeal. The cheap painting was a cover for the real deal. *Oh please. It had to be.*

I held my breath as I removed the frame. Taped to the back of the painting, I found a sealed envelope addressed to *Rosie*. My father's handwriting. I stuffed it in my pocket and commenced to peeling away layers of Key West in bright acrylic colors.

After the final layer, I sat and marveled. I never understood art or why someone would spend five hundred, let alone five million on a painting. But the Falcon mesmerized me.

The bird was in flight with its prey—a terrified grey mouse—in his beak, and wings expanded. Its talons seemed to glitter, sharp as knives. The artist captured the determination in the bird's eyes as he clung to his meal.

Now I understood all those lengthy art conversations my father and his colleagues used to have. Prior to him being a felonious dealer, dad was a legitimate lover of fine artwork and appreciated the artists. He would say, "Rosebud, the pain and suffering of the artist is revealed in their work."

The thought of The Falcon in the hands of this sick SOB revolted me.

I knew what I had to do.

CHAPTER 43

J ames sat at the table, reviewing all he'd learned from Kevin when a heavy knock startled him. "Who is it?" He jumped off the chair.

"Hey, Powers. It's Titos."

"Crap ... uh ... one sec, I ... I'm not decent. Just got out of the shower." James grabbed his gun and put it in his ankle holster. He ran to the sink and wet his hair and placed a towel around his collar. He texted O'Malley. *Titos here. Hurry.*

Titos banged again.

James cracked the door. "Hey, what's up?"

As he pushed his way in, Titos scanned the room and peeked his head in the bathroom.

"What the hell?" James snapped.

"Who's in here with ya? I heard someone

talking."

"I was on the phone ... and how long have you been standing here?"

Titos glared at James with his hands on his hips. "I thought you were in the shower?"

"What the fuck is this? 50 questions? Back off, Titos!"

"Look here asshole, it's Agent Titianos to you and you're in my house now." Titos puffed his chest and drew in closer. "I'll ask the questions," he said through gnashed teeth.

James shoved him. "Get off my ass, *Titos*, it's not *your* jurisdiction. I know all about you." He jammed his finger in Titos's chest. "I can smell a dirty cop a mile away. And you reek. I know you're working for that piece of shit, Max. You're a disgrace to the bureau!"

Titos swatted his finger. "Yeah, I guess ya figured me out. *Boy Scout*." He swung and caught James off guard with a right to the jaw.

Titos may have been taller with a bigger build, but James was nimbler and in better shape. James shook it off and returned with a rapid right and even quicker left. He pulled Titos's shoulders in and kneed him in the stomach.

"You fight like a wuss." Titos let out a puff of air as he raised both arms and landed on James, forcing his face to the floor. James rolled out from under and bolted up like a ninja. He stood with a bladed stance and charged Titos, crashing into the dresser and knocking over the lamp. James twirled behind Titos and applied a choke hold.

Suddenly, the door flung open, hitting the wall. "Took you long enough," Titos gurgled.

Crockett emerged with a needle and jammed James in the neck.

"What the fu ..." James slapped his neck and swayed side to side, collapsing in Crockett's arms. "Shit, give me a hand," he grunted.

Titos held up James's right arm. "Let's get him in the car before anyone sees. And grab his keys, I don't want his body in our vehicles. We'll leave yours here."

"Got 'em. Oh, by the way, the lobby's full of a convention of middle-aged paper salesmen. We're going to have to take the stairs."

"You fuckin' kiddin' me?!" Titos growled.

CHAPTER 44

Saki's stomach cramped. She wasn't ready to die, not today. Desperate, she blurted, "I need to go to the bathroom."

Max stopped, gestured to the drain in the corner.

"No, the other."

He rolled his eyes, sighed, and strode away. She'd noticed Max did not discuss bodily functions or anything very distasteful. As he stepped out of the chamber, he waved at someone. Probably a hired hand to take care of her.

A few seconds later the door flung wide. A man took up the entire doorframe.

Max had told her all about Douglas O'Glosson, a.k.a., D.O.G. He was an Irish battering ram of a man and towered at six feet six inches with a close cropped, bright crimson tipped haircut. He was thirty-one and a former center for the Miami Dolphins. In his late twenties he'd sustained a career-ending brain injury.

D.O.G. was another of Max's recruits who owed money to the wrong people. Max hired him after his career ended with the Dolphins.

"Come with me," D.O.G. boomed.

Saki's jaw dropped at the sheer size of him. She followed, speechless. They made their way up the concrete stairwell into the foyer. Left was freedom. She turned that way, but D.O.G. herded her right.

The mansion had shiny, white marble floors, with a black and gold welded hand railing. There were paintings and statues Saki had only seen the likes of in museums.

"It's down the hall." D.O.G. pointed.

She closed the door and tried to lock the knob, but discovered there was no lock. She rushed to the window and pushed, but it had been nailed shut from the outside.

"Shit, shit, shit."

She paced the small room. "I'm not going back there. Think, Saki ..."

CHAPTER 45

Out here, due process is a bullet! John Wayne's quote popped in my brain as I loaded my backpack with extra mags and shoved my Kahr P380 into my back-up bra holster. I packed my car twice and paced a hole in the carpet as I waited for the exchange instructions.

I turned on the noon news to get Max out of my head and breathed a sigh of relief there weren't any reports of a crazed red-haired crypt robber. As I changed the channel, my phone vibrated. "Mother ... breathe, Rose." I exhaled.

Max rescheduled our meet and greet to eight. An uneasiness fell over me.

As I cursed his existence, a crash shook my room.

Lightning? From an approaching storm? But

another followed too quickly.

I shut off the TV and listened.

Men above me yelled, and bodies thrashed. One voice sounded familiar.

It was him! My midnight intruder. The crooked cop. Max's goon. His voice added fuel to the raging fire in my gut. *But why was he here?*

The answer came when I peeked out the drapes and spotted the cop and his associate escorting a third man down the stairs. I overheard the dirt bag call his chum Crockett. They swung on the landing, and my heart stopped.

"No. Not James!" I muffled my scream with my hand. The men dragged my sedated partner by his arms and struggled to stuff him in the rear seat of a white Cavalier. Outlaw cop jumped in a black Chevy Tahoe. I could spot a government undercover vehicle a mile away with its lights embedded in the grill. It didn't surprise me he used it for his other job.

As I ran out of the motel room with my backpack, I snapped a picture of his G ride and raced after them.

My sister? Now my best friend!

Darkness crashed over me.

"Someone's gonna die today."

CHAPTER 46

Heavy sheets of rain fell over the roadway as I trailed them out of Key West onto US-1 North, maintaining two car lengths behind while dialing 911. My right hand bore nail impressions from the vice grip on the steering wheel and my heart pulsated in my arm still suspended in the sling. As we crossed the Overseas Highway, my cheap burner phone dropped the 911 dispatcher.

Just as we passed the Naval Air Station and Rockland Key, they made an abrupt left on Shark Road, and zagged to the right, onto Croc Lane. I recognized it from childhood stories. The area was home to hungry crocodiles and known only to the local dirtbags as quick human disposal. In Godfather's terms, they were "sleeping with the fishes." But in the glades, it's the crocs.

James's captors drove down a sloped one-way road and parked at the bottom near the edge of the lagoon and jumped out, leaving their cars running. They yanked James out of the Cavalier and stood him at the shore of the swamp.

I pulled in and hid my car behind a row of orange Geiger trees at the top of the ravine and headed down the embankment with my backpack.

James struggled to stand and swayed as he cursed them. I cringed. It was only a matter of time before the crocs took notice lunch was being served.

"Okay, Boy Scout, it's the end of the line for ya. No hard feelings, huh?" The dirty cop scoffed.

"Come on, Titosh," James slurred.

"Titos, that's his name," I whispered with a clenched jaw.

Titos snickered at James and drew his 40 caliber Sig Sauer from his shoulder holster as Crockett stood back to back with him. He extended a long metal rod with a hoop on the end and was on croc duty. The two men were no strangers to body dumping.

"You don't have to do this. I won't tell anyone. I promise." James's voice shook as he waved his hands.

"Bullshit! You'll rat the second I let ya go! Besides, Max gave me orders. But hey, no worries, you won't be alone for long. As soon as Max gets the Falcon, a feisty blonde will join ya."

Titos raised his pistol.

CHAPTER 47

"**S**top! Drop the gun, asshole!" I screamed as I slid half-way down the ridge.

They jerked their heads in my direction. Crockett's and Titos's mouths hung open and James wore a grin of relief.

"Sorry, Rose, you're too late." Titos returned his attention to James. "Crockett, deal with her," he said.

As Crockett fired at me, Titos shot James, hitting him center mass.

"*No!*" I dropped to the ground, took cover behind a tree and peppered both men. I found myself in another slow-motion movie as James and Titos propelled backward and disappeared into the marsh. Crockett continued shooting at me as he escaped in Titos's ride, kicking up rocks on his way out.

The commotion stirred two hungry residents. Crocodiles snap with thousands of pounds of force and have a mean bite. Reptile's jaws are not wired to masticate their food. They can only chomp and rip off sizeable chunks of their prey and swallow them whole, letting their stomachs do the work. They sometimes drown their meal and let it sit and rot before they eat it. Not these two.

Titos was first. He howled as one snapped his arm, dragged, and rolled him. I could hear bones crunching. As I slid the rest of the way down the embankment on my backside, I ejected my magazine. *Please, God.* Slammed the new one against my thigh to insert it. I was becoming a pro at being a one-armed bandit. Help me, God.

My blood pressure doubled as I landed with one foot in the swamp, the other in the sand. *God, now please! I need you!* I rapidly unloaded my weapon on both crocs, but it was futile. After one took off with Titos, the other slithered to James and snatched his shirt. Blood filled the mucky waters. He vanished.

I ran to the other side and saw James's tan FBI polo torn and crimson colored. "*No! James!*" I screamed.

I bolted back and forth, hoping for a visual, but nothing.

My body was heavy with defeat as I sobbed my way to the rental. I peered over my shoulder, searching for signs of life.

All was quiet. Then a few bubbles surfaced.

I held my breath, waiting. But nothing more.

This was my fault, all of it.

I couldn't breathe, the guilt suffocated me. I should have confided in James. *Don't be stubborn. Ask for help*, he'd tell me. But I didn't know how.

My father was to blame. His last words before they escorted him out in handcuffs. *Be Daddy's brave little superhero and take care of Mommy and your sister*. It etched in my memory and became my identity.

My incessant need to be the crusader was my Kryptonite. "I'm not your damn little superhero, Dad. I failed," I shouted and shook the wheel with a death grip. "I failed them all! And where were you, God? I needed you!"

Tears surged like the ocean's waves, one after the other. And then it stung me like a Man o' War. I was never angry at my father for leaving me, for leaving us, until now.

I took off wallowing in a self-loathing pool of regret.

CHAPTER 48

"**U**m, Doggie. Here, Doggie." Saki jeered as she poked her head out of the bathroom.

"It's D.O.G.," he boomed, approaching down the hall. "Dee. Oh. Gee."

"Yeah, sorry. I have a problem. It's kinda embarrassing." She scrunched her nose.

"What?" he snapped.

Most men were uncomfortable with the menses conversation, a fact she counted on now. "I started my period and don't have any tampons or pads or ..."

"Ah, shit." He placed both hands on his hips. "Okay ... I'll be right back." He rushed down the hall and howled. "Heidi ... Max!" He patted his pockets for his phone. "Crap, it's in my car." He hurried back to the bathroom. "Stay!" He held his hand to her as if she were the dog. "So help me, if you try to escape, I'll shoot ya myself."

Saki held a smirk as he flustered. She had no plan but needed time. After he yelled his way up the stairs, she ducked inside and searched every maple wood cabinet. "Come on, there's got to be something." She leaned on the sink and talked to herself in the oval-shaped mirror. It wasn't just a mirror, but a medicine cabinet.

She opened it. "I can use this." Just as she stuffed it between her ankle sock and Reebok, she heard a light knock at the door.

"Hello?" said a soothing, familiar voice on the other side.

Saki cracked it opened.

A woman in her late sixties, matronly with gray hair and worn out green eyes stood there. "I'm Heidi Zimm. I hear you need …" She glanced at D.O.G. and back to Saki. "Pads." She covered her mouth and whispered.

"Uh … yeah." Saki stumbled over her words. "Do I know you?" She opened the door wider.

Heidi studied her.

CHAPTER 49

"I'm Saki." With a half-hearted smile, she shook Heidi's hand.

D.O.G. interrupted. "Ladies, let's save the tea party for later and take care of business."

"Saki? That's unique. I only knew one other person with that na ...." She stopped as Saki shook her head. "Uh ... I'm sorry, but I don't have any products for you. I'm way past that time in my life. Ha, thank God." Her voice shuddered as she laughed. "I can run to the market ... but, I um ... left my purse upstairs."

Heidi turned her gaze up to D.O.G. "Douglas, can you be a dear and get it for me, please? It is in my room." D.O.G. visibly melted as she called him by his birth name.

"Yes, ma'am." He spoke like a loving son to

his mother.

Heidi watched D.O.G. walk away. She returned to Saki with tears in her eyes. "Saki? Honey. Is that really you?" She cupped Saki's face in her hands. "The last time I saw you, you were two. You and your family would spend weekends with Max and his parents at the beach house. But ... but what in the heck are you doing here?" she asked in a hushed voice, "with Max?"

Saki closed her eyes and drew a deep breath to hold back the tidal wave of emotions surging. She remembered Heidi's loving voice. It was the same as her talking Mrs. Beasley doll she had as a child. She would cuddle Mrs. Beasley while Heidi lulled her to sleep. She'd worked as Max's nanny since he was a child.

Saki squeezed Heidi in a hug and whispered with a muffled cry. "Ma ... Max kidnapped me. He's going to kill me. Please help."

"What! Max? Oh my, we have to get you out of here." Heidi pulled away from Saki and handed her a tissue from her pocket. "I never thought I'd see you or Rose again. I stayed on after Max's mother's death, as a personal favor to him. Since I never married, nor had any children, Max is like my own. I oversee the household, but Max keeps me in the dark with his business dealings. I suspected he had a shady side, but I ignored it. Until now."

"Be careful, he's dangerous." Saki wiped her face.

Heidi glared up the stairs. "Don't worry about me. I know how to handle Maxwell."

CHAPTER 50

James shot up like a rocket out of the south end of the swamp, gasping for air and flailing his arms. "Sto ..." He struggled to purge the water from his lungs as she sped away. He glanced at the carnage and jumped at a set of black, vacant eyes easing its way toward him. A moment of relief fell over him when it coiled over, belly up and bleeding.

As he paddled to the shore, he passed crocodile number two, oblivious to his presence and blissfully chomping lunch. His heart pounded as he reached the safety of the shoreline, grateful the croc didn't take notice of his escaping dessert.

James dropped to his knees at the top of the sandy hill and puked up slimy swamp water. As he rolled onto his back, he patted himself twice to make sure his appendages were intact. He stared up to the heavens and beamed. He spied a small patch of baby blue sky tucked in between the gray clouds.

For a split second, he thought he saw them form the shape of an angel. He didn't go to church anymore. Twelve years of parochial school was more than he could handle. But today his faith was restored. Out of nowhere a bible verse from Psalms popped in his brain. *Where does my help come from? My help comes from the Lord, the Maker of heaven and earth.* He winked. "Thank you, Big Guy, I owe you!"

He grunted as he stood and assessed his swamp-soaked, shredded clothing. Just then an ooze dripped from his thigh. He peeked down and found a piece of flesh hanging. He tore off what remained of his shirt and tied it above the bite mark. "Argh!" He howled and hobbled up the embankment to his rental.

"Croc wrestling is something they didn't cover in the academy. Guess I can add that to my resume," James mumbled as he retrieved the hemostatic agent from the trauma kit in his trunk.

"I *was* a Boy Scout, you mother fucker. I'm always prepared." He turned and screamed through gritted teeth at his half-eaten counterpart. He sat on his bumper and applied the Quick Clot to stop his hemorrhage.

"I have been through some crazy shit, but this takes the cake." He winced as he took off his ballistic vest and inspected his bruised torso. "Now I know what Rose meant. It does feel like a baseball bat."

James stared at the crime scene in the water when an intense buzzing startled him. He let out a loud gust of air when he realized it was his cell phone and not another approaching croc. He followed the noise and located it wedged between the rear seat where his captors had stuffed his body.

O'Malley. He swiped to answer the call. "Hey, bud—sorry, I was detained. I just crawled out of the swamp with a croc—no, I am not bullshitting you. Yep, I got a welcome committee at my hotel. Your boy with one of Max's goons snatched me and tried to whack me. Mm hm, nope, he won't be a problem anymore, he's in the intestines of a croc—ha, yeah, he's got a different kind of internal investigation going on.

"But, uh, I need a favor. I'm kinda half naked here and I am preeety sure I am not supposed to be bleeding this much—no, I'm fine. But can you stop by my room and pick up my black bag ... oh, and more body armor."

James tossed his bullet-riddled vest into the car.

CHAPTER 51

Max listened to Crockett recount what happened at the swamp without comment until the end.

"I should tell her thank you. It saved me the job of doing it myself. Titos was a fuck-up, anyway." Max leaned back in his soft brown leather chair behind his mahogany desk and studied Crockett. He jerked when he observed a red substance dripped from Crockett's arm. "What the hell, man! You're bleeding on my new desk." He removed a tissue from the box and handed it over. "It's a good thing Rose hit you with just one round. Did you at least find her room and search it?"

Crockett looked sideways at Max and popped. "I'm fucking shot. How was I going to do that? I drove straight here. I'm your pilot, not your hired lackey." He peeked at his leaking arm under the gauze and applied more pressure. "I think I need to get this checked."

"Yeah, yeah, okay." Max turned. "D.O.G.! Get in here."

D.O.G. was at the door in seconds, carrying Heidi's purse over his shoulder. "What the hell! What are you doing up here? And what are you holding?"

"Well ... uh ... Saki needed some ... uh ... female supplies. Heidi's gonna go get 'em, but she needed her purse."

"You left Heidi alone with her? Are you out of your mind?"

"Sorry Max ... I ... I didn't know." D.O.G. stared at his shoes.

"Get Heidi up here now! Oh, and call your girlfriend ..." Max snapped his fingers. "That nurse."

"Lucy." D.O.G. picked his head up and blushed. He grinned ear to ear at the sound of her name.

Max didn't waste his time on trivial things like remembering people's names unless it benefited him. But Lucy was not just any nurse. She worked as an on-call at a nearby clinic, though lately she spent more time patching up gunshot wounds on Max's people. He paid her well, and in return, she was tight lipped with the local cops. D.O.G. met her a few years ago when she first stitched him. It was love at first sight.

"Uh ... what do I do about the girl?"

"The boatshed, D.O.G.!" Max ordered. "As

soon as you're patched, you two get it ready. Take a picture of the girl and send it to this number." Max scribbled the digits and handed it to D.O.G.

CHAPTER 52

My soul was heavy with grief as I drove back to Key West.

I dialed Kaylee the second I had cell service and sobbed every detail of my hellish afternoon. She said again that we needed to talk, so I asked her to meet me at my happy place as a kid, the Key West City Park.

When I pulled in, memories poured over me like sweet coconut milk. The park rested on ten acres of rich green grass surrounded by palm trees swaying in the cool sea breeze. The dazzling shooting star shrubs bordered the front while the back faced the ocean.

There were benches at every curve. Snowy egrets, with their elegant black legs and bright yellow feet, scampered about and pelicans fed off the shore.

As I made my way around the concrete path, I stumbled across the gazebo in the center where my summer crush, Sammy, etched our initials in the shape of a heart. I found it among all the other broken promises carved here.

Sammy was smitten with me. In his fantasy land, we were soul mates. But what does any eleven-year-old know about forever? I often thought of him over the years and whatever became of him. After the shooting, we were sent away and lost touch. Never to speak again.

I continued my journey and searched every park bench until I found it. The one where my mom and Vivian, Sammy's mother, would chat for hours as they watched the three of us build sandcastles. We never asked or cared about their conversations, but there were tears and laughter. Knowing our fathers, I can only surmise they vented about their husbands and the shady business dealings of M.T. Art Galleries.

As I sat and rested my weary eyes, the salty sea mist sprayed my face. I could taste it on my lips. The ocean is cathartic, it hears our woes and keeps our secrets. I drew a long meditative breath and a sudden gust carried in a discernable floral bouquet, like my mother's. A reassuring ease enveloped me. I peered up, and a smile crept in one corner of my mouth. Her spirit was alive.

Just as I went to stand, the envelope fell from my back pocket. The one from The Falcon's frame. In the morning's haste, I'd forgotten it.

My eyes widened as I read it. Then I sighed and shook my head as I set it on my lap. "Why doesn't it surprise me?"

Is this what she wanted to discuss? How long has she known?

Kaylee's arrival interrupted my thoughts. As she ran up to me, the look on her face answered my question.

"I always wished for a sister. Now I have two."

She sobbed.

CHAPTER 53

Heidi took her last order from Max. She often wondered why he would give her a week's paid vacation to any destination of her choosing. She assumed it was payback for raising the spoiled brat. Now she understood. It was to keep her from the shady, criminal side of his life. The thugs he had on his payroll made sense to her.

As Max smiled and peeled off two twenties from the roll of bills in his pocket, he told her to go buy supplies for Saki, but just to drop them off at the guard shack at the front gate. Then she could take the rest of the week off and head up to Hilton Head. He'd make a reservation.

After D.O.G. ushered her out of Max's office, she eavesdropped and held her mouth as she gasped at their plan. She rushed to her room and packed her bag.

Heidi loaded her car and slammed the door. She looked up to be sure he heard her depart. He waved from his office window. She waved back and hopped into the driver's seat.

But instead of leaving the property, she drove to the south end of the servants' quarters and parked out of sight.

D.O.G. and Crockett were arguing as she tiptoed past the garage.

"I don't know, D.O.G. Titos was supposed to deal with this cell phone explosive shit. I am just a freaking pilot." Crockett sounded more frustrated than angry.

Heidi held her breath as she stealthily walked the three yards over the rickety boat dock, into the shed.

She ran to Saki and removed her gag. "We need to hurry."

"Thank you so much, Heidi. You took a big risk coming in here. I owe you my life," Saki said, teary eyed as she wrestled with her restraints.

"I'm sorry we had to see one another again under such dreadful conditions." Heidi fumbled with the rope. "A key to the rear door is hanging behind the lighthouse picture. When you get out, swim to the south as far as you can go. I'll be waiting."

Saki nodded and wiggled to free her legs. "I took something from the bathroom that might help." Just as Saki lifted her shoe, the door burst open.

"What the hell are you doing?" Crockett demanded.

"You boys should be ashamed of yourselves," Heidi barked and shot a disapproving scowl between them.

Crockett ran to her and grabbed her arm. "You're coming with me, Grandma. Max is gonna be pissed. He gave you one opportunity to take off, now it's too late."

"Leave her alone! She did nothing to you guys," Saki said.

Crockett pulled Heidi out the door with a forceful yank.

"Don't hurt her, you ass ho—" D.O.G. gagged Saki again and tightened her ropes.

"Look at me," he said.

Saki glared daggers as he took her picture.

CHAPTER 54

Kaylee and I had an instant connection the moment we met. This explained so much.

"So, your mother was a nurse at the federal pen and hooked up with my ... uh ... our father? And here we are." My lip curled.

"Yep. They conceived me in prison." She stared off and shook her head.

"So, tell me. Is he alive?"

Kaylee shrugged. "Not sure, I never met him. I found out today after I hammered Uncle Tubbs with questions." She sat next to me. "Uncle T had been in contact with him until three months ago."

"Three months ...?" My mind raced. We'd been told he died in prison. "What made you question Tubbs?"

"My uncle doesn't do favors for just anyone. There had to be something special about you."

We listened to the crashing waves and spoke at the same time.

I patted her leg. "You first."

"I'm sorry, Rose."

"For what? It's not your fault our father was a lying, cheating, criminal. At least I was born in the free world." We looked at each other and chuckled. "Sorry, Kaylee. But, boy ... I'd like to give him a piece of my mind." I shook my head. "We can talk about dear daddy later. It's time to get my—err, uh, our sister back." I stood. "But we can't do it alone."

"We don't have to." Kaylee grinned. And she explained.

Her boyfriend, Ray, was a cop with the Key West Police Department and on duty this evening. He told Kaylee he was working a "secret squirrel mission" with the feds. I felt deep in my heart and soul my late colleague initiated the operation before his untimely demise. Tears welled up and my stomach sank at the thought of James and how I'd never again call him AP and he'd have a comeback for Felicity. I choked back a sob. God, I'd miss him.

As I lamented, my phone buzzed with a text from an unknown number. Another picture of Saki, tied up.

"What the hell? No! This can't be, how ... why?" I paced in front of Kaylee. "Oh my God! The boatshed, and ... that painting."

She shot me a sideways look.

I sat again and threw my arm around my

new sister. "Kaylee! I know where Saki is being held. And Max's real identity!"

CHAPTER 55

After D.O.G. left, Saki waited a few moments. She fumbled as she twisted her wrists and legs. A grin formed. Thank God he was a few bricks short of a full load. D.O.G. didn't tie her ankles together. He bound each one to a chair leg, allowing her free to move.

Saki picked her head up and peered out the window. No one there. She removed her left shoe and flung it back with her foot to her hand and pulled out the straight-edge razor blade she'd appropriated from the bathroom.

She held her gaze on the door and began severing the rope. But the humidity made for a slippery grip, and she sliced the upper part of her thumb. The sweat dripped from under her armpit and into her fresh wound. "Ffuu." She muffled her scream and panted. Saki had never taken Lamaze classes, but she'd heard enough to be able to use the breathing technique.

Male voices approached. She sneaked a look but ducked as Crockett scanned her direction. He saw her. She glanced behind her chair, saw droplets of blood. She shifted to conceal the bright red evidence and position herself in front of the painting, where they left her. She held her breath until the door opened. But it didn't.

The men got closer because their voices grew louder.

D.O.G. spoke. "Max needs you to babysit and set the charge. I'm gonna greet his guest. I'll text you when it's time. Remember, run like hell."

Heavy footsteps sounded, D.O.G. leaving Crockett behind to guard her. Saki forced herself to take slow, easy breaths. She could still do this. She *had* to do this.

CHAPTER 56

Special Agent in Charge Kevin O'Malley commanded respect as he conducted his multi-agency briefing of law enforcement officers from Key West, Miami-Dade, and his own FBI team.

"After weapons and drug trafficking, art theft is the largest criminal enterprise in the world. The FBI's art loss database registers half a million pieces. These are either lost, stolen, or reported with authenticity issues. Yet the full extent of the illegal art market is unknown. Approximately 50,000 to 100,000 works are appropriated each year."

He lectured from the back using a red laser pointer at his slide show presentation. "These items are often smuggled, internationally traded, and/or kept in private homes, collecting dust. Only becoming public when they are sold through auctions and legitimate markets."

O'Malley handed out the ops plan. "Folks, our target, Maxwell Ryan, A.K.A., Samuel Alexander is the real deal. He is Richie Rich loaded. He was a trust-fund kid whose mother came from a prominent New York family. He owns homes all over the world, including Hawaii, Italy, and the French Riviera. Over half of his assets are legit, the rest are from felonious activities. He inherited that gene from his dad.

"I have reason to believe he has three of the thirty paintings that went missing from the Gardner Museum in Boston. Among them are a Rembrandt, a Manet, and a Vermeer. None of these have surfaced since the heist. Also, a Van Gogh was lifted from a collector's home in Italy last year. Ironically, Mr. Ryan owns a villa nearby. We don't have firm evidence because all our witnesses mysteriously vanished or are tight lipped."

A twenty-something year old local cop interrupted. "Excuse me sir, but what does this have to do with the kidnapping?"

"That brings me to my next point." He shot an annoyed look at the youngster. "Saki's abduction is our foot in the door. After her safe extraction, we will hopefully get the evidence we need to justify a more invasive warrant."

The same cop raised his hand and nervously asked. "Sir, why was Saki kidnapped?"

"The O'Brien sisters have possession of a

rare painting. It's the final piece of the Hawk Trilogy. Max has the first two." He clicked to the next slide. "The Falcon alone is worth five million." He glanced around the room.

"I don't get it. If this guy is so wealthy, why does he care about a five-million-dollar picture?" a female FBI agent inquired.

"I'm not certain. Sometimes the financial value of an object is inconsequential if there is a personal connection. There is history between our target and the O'Brien women. I've got a theory the Falcon is personal.

"First, we need confirmation of Saki's location. I know Ryan has a couple residences." He strolled to the front, rolled up the screen and revealed the white board with addresses and photos of Max, Saki, and Rose. "We'll have two teams—"

The rear door flung open.

CHAPTER 57

"**T**hat's not the correct location," I blurted and pushed through the crowded, stuffy briefing room.

Twenty cops dressed in black tactical gear sat with gaped mouths as I made my way to the front. Their heads moved in unison as they studied the series of pictures and returned their gaze to me. I didn't know if they viewed me as a rogue agent or victim.

The agent up front pursed his lips. "Let's take five, folks." A six-foot-and some change, salt and peppered haired man folded his arms across his broad chest. He wore 511 khaki tactical pants and a black polo shirt that bore the FBI emblem.

My heart fluttered and chills ran through my body as he approached. His sea-green eyes caught me off guard. Neither of us spoke for a millisecond.

He cleared his throat. "Good evening, Rose. Special Agent in Charge Kevin O'Malley with the Miami FBI." He reached out and the second we touched, electricity surged.

"I ... I'm sorry for interrupting." I stammered and looked away. *He's not your late husband. Shake it off, Rose.*

Just then, my picture tacked to the wall captured my attention. I removed it and inspected it. "Why has this been folded a million times?" I gave him a puzzled look.

He snatched it away and ignored my question. "We have confirmation this is Max's address." He pointed to the map. What do you have different?" He was back to business.

"You're partially correct." I took out my burner cell and showed him Saki's picture. "This is where she is being held. That house—" I pointed to the map— "is on the other side of the keys."

"Are you sure?"

"You see this boatshed?"

"And?" He made a go on motion with one hand.

Unquestionably, not my Bradley. This guy's a butthead. "I stayed there as a kid. Besides." I zoomed in on the painting behind Saki. "My crayon contribution. I was Picasso at five."

"O. Kay." He enunciated each letter. "I need more than a five-year-old's artwork for a warrant."

"It's unnecessary," I said with a raised

eyebrow. "I'm an invited guest. I don't recall the exact address, somewhere on Ocean, it's at the end of a cul-de-sac. Asshole hasn't given me digits, yet. He's playing a sick and twisted game."

"Agent O'Brien, with all due respect, you have no jurisdiction here. Furthermore, you're too involved in this case." He motioned to my bloody, dirty sling. "And are in no condition to assist." He placed his hands on his hips and glared as if I'd peed in his Cheerios.

I drew a long, deep breath. "First, I'm no longer an agent. I turned in my badge and ID. Second, Max invited me. I can walk in the front door and grab a cup of coffee." I exhaled. "And I know you're itching to get him on other charges, but he took my sister." I pounded my chest and raised the octane in my voice. "Right now, I could give a rat's ass about your art pieces!" Silence fell in the room.

"I wouldn't argue with her. She makes a compelling case." A recognizable voice emerged from the crowd and my heart stopped for two beats. "Besides, I've tried many times. She can be a stubborn brat."

James stepped out from the crowd. "And Agent O'Brien, you didn't turn in your badge. I held onto it for safe keep—"

CHAPTER 58

"James?" I whispered, walking toward him on rubbery legs. "How ... how the hell did ... your shirt had blood and ..." I wrapped my arms around him, buried my face in his neck and wept.

After a long moment, he loosened my bear hug and stepped back. "Thanks to your mad shooting skills, partner. I'm here and in one piece." He glanced at his thigh. "Well, almost." And chuckled.

James told me his croc wrestling story and Titos's bloody ending. I couldn't stop staring at him. My partner, AP to my Felicity, was alive. He'd survived a crocodile attack. I drew a shaky breath and listened to his deep voice tell everyone it was thanks to me shooting the croc, but I knew the truth: somehow, someway God heard and answered my desperate prayer on the edge of that swamp.

After our ten-minute reunion, we returned to business.

"Felicity, I agree with Kevin. It's too risky to go alone."

"AP, trust me, I'm not trying to be a hero."

"Yeah, sure." Agent O'Malley snarked. "I've heard about you. I'm surprised you're not at Max's gate with your guns blazing."

"Okay, I deserve that, but no more."

"What?" James drawled. "Do my ears deceive me, Felicity?"

I shot him a closed mouth grin. "We can't go in hot. His goon, Titos, paid me a midnight visit when you came to town, AP. Our fists did most of the talking." I rubbed my shoulder. "He accused me of bringing in the cops. If he sees you all, he won't hesitate to kill Saki. Besides, I have something he wants."

"The Falcon." James exchanged glances with O'Malley.

"So ... you both know?"

James nodded and sighed.

"Sorry, partner. No more secrets. I'll tell you everything later. Right now, it's time to rescue your girlfriend." I winked. "Don't look at me that way, I see a twinkle in your eye every time Saki's name comes up."

After I pled my case, we all agreed.

I'd walk through the front door.

CHAPTER 59

A wave of nausea brewed in Saki's stomach as she watched Crockett adjust the charge. She wasn't sure if it was caused by the humidity or her pending doom. She finished fraying the last bit of rope that loosely bound her leg and then crawled toward the lighthouse painting.

Pinching the wires between her thumbs and index fingers, she cringed when it slipped and crashed to the floor. "Crap!" she muttered.

She snatched the key, stuffed it in her pocket, and returned to the chair. Her heart raced as she hurried to retie her legs, but it was too late for her wrists.

Just as he rushed inside, she bolted upright, holding her hands behind her.

"What was that?" Crockett scanned the room.

"A huge lizard knocked it off the wall." She nodded toward the painting, trying to keep her breathing even, not like she'd run a marathon in her sweat-soaked tankini.

"What are you up to?" He frowned.

"Noth ... nothing. Hey, you know it's hotter than shit in here. Can you open the windows?"

"Nope." He shook his head. "They stay closed. Max warned me about you. I don't want you sneaking out. And what's in your hands?" He moved toward her.

"Aargh!" She bolted forward in her seat.

"What the hell is wrong with you?" Crockett stopped and scowled.

"I told you, the heat's getting to me!" She arched, pressing her breasts out. "Please, may I have water? I'm so thirsty," she said in her most seductive voice.

"Is that all you got? My girlfriend's a Dolphin's cheerleader with a bigger rack. Nice try." Crockett scoffed and scanned the area. "Saki, you won't need water." He exited and clicked the padlock.

"Prick," she mumbled and glared.

As soon as he left, she shucked off the leg ties again, then tiptoed to the rear door, floorboards creaking with every step.

She removed the key and slid it into the hole, but it was corroded from decades of sea air. She held her breath and inch by inch she turned it.

"Almost there."

Snap.

"No!"

CHAPTER 60

As the sun began its final descent, I sat at the stop sign on Coconut and Palm Street. The memories flooded me, again.

Over twenty years ago I'd roamed these narrow streets, carefree. Key West in a simpler, innocent era. I peered to my left and spied the treehouse where I had my first attempted kiss.

The home was residence to an elderly, wealthy couple whose names escaped me. They produced a children's show in Miami, something about a dolphin. They had no time for kids of their own, so they erected a huge three-room treehouse for the locals.

My first crush and I used to play Tarzan in their backyard. Our wild imaginations took us places. One summer, jungle people kidnapped my sweetie. I rescued him, and in return, he leaned in with his lips. I wasn't ready and popped him in the jaw.

After seeing the deflated expression on his face, I ran to my mother, who gave me the birds and bees lecture. She also told me boys need to be the hero. Total opposite of what my father taught me.

I was a tomboy and didn't buy the damsel-in-distress routine, but I liked him and played the game. The next abduction, I allowed him to come to my aid and planted one on him. The rest of the summer, we were an item.

An impatient driver, honking, interrupted my little jaunt. I'd overstayed my welcome on memory lane. As I passed the house, it occurred to me our naïve childhood imagination had become a sick, twisted reality.

I was on my way to rescue my sister from my first crush, turned psychopath. I should have let the jungle people keep him.

CHAPTER 61

O 'Malley gave me and James a quick briefing.

Max's water-front mansion sat on three and a half acres at the end of an ultra-private cul-de-sac. His Fort Knox-worthy security system and ten-foot concrete walls posed a surveillance challenge for the multi-agency task force. Thus making a surprise raid next to impossible.

This is where the harbor patrol came into play. To the untrained eye, the first boat to motor by, comprised of a young couple entwined in one another's embrace out for a sunset cruise and piloted by a bored owner who made this trek a million times shouldn't arouse suspicion.

But a closer look would reveal the quizzical

love birds posed as undercover officers doing recon work with a team of federal agents prepped in the lower deck, waiting to spring on their unwary adversary. If everything went according to plan.

The subsequent boats were equipped with the Key West Harbor Patrol's lights and sirens.

The fed's brainiacs outfitted me with a special hidden earpiece concealed by my hair band. We had two-way audio communication, but no visual. A camera was too detectable. My task was to provide enough ammunition for more than a kidnapping charge.

The feds salivated at Max's property like a wild pack of dogs on raw meat. Kevin O'Malley's favorite two words, *asset forfeiture*, resonated in my head.

As I pulled up, he chirped in my ear. "Okay, Red. I'm counting on your keen eye." He called me Red, which irked me. James told me O'Malley gave nicknames to people he liked. He said if I wanted a real job, I could switch sides and he would take me on in his unit. I was not amused.

I had one thing on my mind: distract Max so the team could execute Saki's rescue.

That was the plan.

But plans change.

CHAPTER 62

Adrenaline surged through my veins as the surveillance camera followed my every movement from the entrance to the front gate.

"He's already got eyes on me." I spoke through a wide smile.

"Drive forward." I flinched at the loud boom from the intercom. The gates swung open and I inched through. I followed a curving drive through aged palmettos and finally stopped in front of huge, double front doors.

As I exited my car, a refrigerator of a man greeted me.

"Hi, I'm Ro—" I strained my neck as I scanned him.

"I know who you are." His voice matched the body. He spun me around and started his thorough pat-down for weapons.

"Hey, easy there," I shot over my shoulder as his hands drew closer to my chest. "Second base and no kiss first?" I snarked as he worked his way in between my thighs.

"I see where Saki gets her sarcasm." He grunted as he finished checking my ankles. Thank God he missed my bra holster.

"Where is she?" I demanded.

"Falcon first," he replied, straight-faced.

I sneered and nodded to the Malibu. "My sister?"

"Downstairs, with Max." He pointed to the doors that opened on cue.

"Red, you giving up the Falcon that easy?" O'Malley quirked.

"Nope," I murmured. "Did you copy that? Something's wrong. Standby and wait for confirmation."

I stopped in my tracks at the threshold, goose bumps the size of mountains. The marble flooring echoed beneath my every step. I ran a hand along the custom-made railing with intricate metal vines as I started down the staircase to the lower level. I didn't recall it being so formal. As kids, we'd slid down a wood bannister. This was all familiar ... yet, not.

"Speak to me, Red."

I looked at the paintings lining the staircase. "Wow, is this a Vermeer? I've only seen this in ... *pictures*."

"Red, did not ... you."

"I'm losing you guys," I mumbled as I trembled my way down the dirty, unyielding concrete steps.

CHAPTER 63

The musty death odor knocked me off my feet. I peered around my former playroom that was now a scene from Dungeons and Dragons. Soundproof padding replaced the sea scape mural that had covered the walls. I caught my reflection in a one-way mirror. *That's new.* I cocked my head.

As I turned, my heart fluttered. Saki's back was to me, her golden mane draped the rickety chair.

"Baby sister, I am so sorr—" I rushed over and swiveled her seat.

"What the *fuck* is this?"

My body jolted so fast I gave myself whiplash. A life-sized clown's beady eyes stared at me. It wore a long blonde wig and a joker's mocking smile.

The hairs on my arm stood on end and then it hit me.

That familiar, revolting cologne. The same scent that haunted my hospital room and permeated my home was now right behind me.

The door slammed shut. I spun.

Sammy.

CHAPTER 64

The team posted up in a silver delivery van with blackout curtains and parked catty corner from Max's compound, in plain sight. The van was painted with roses and carnations with Mary's Flowers stenciled in subdued pink and white. On any given day it could be disguised as a television repair van or a plumber. But today, a florist. The retractable high-powered radio antenna bore resemblance to a small roof fan.

The van was equipped with a hidden intercom system in the front driver's compartment in the center console to communicate with the agents in the back. Behind the two front seats was a concealed door that served as the entrance to the command center.

The rear sector encompassed two brown rotating captain's chairs, and all the bells and whistles to include a workstation, computers, monitoring equipment, radios, night vision, thermal imaging, GPS video, and more. The agents were chilled by a separate air conditioning system that used dry ice for cooling. But the excessive humidity on this particular evening pushed the system beyond its limits to the point where it spit out 80-degree temps.

"O'Brien! Do you read me?" O'Malley shook his head at James, who sat next to him.

"Crap, we lost her. Did she confirm Vermeer?" His voice went up a note as he tapped on his receiver. "Come on, Rose, speak to me." O'Malley pursed his lips and continued talking to his equipment. "Are you freaking kidding me? All this hi-tech shit and we lose her. Max must have a jamming system, or she's underground.

"Red ... do you copy?" He rotated his chair toward James. "Your partner has to give me more than that for a war—"

"Seriously!" James pounded his armrest. "We lost radio contact and all you care about is your damn affidavit. We've got federal kidnapping charges on this asshole. That's enough for twenty years. What more do you want?"

"Eeeeasy, James. I'm working on it." O'Malley clicked away at the keyboard.

"What the hell are you doing? Did you hear me?" James slammed the laptop screen.

"I know we lost contact. But it's temporary. I sent a message to my geek squad for radio assistance." He reopened the laptop and returned to typing. "Max also has a high-profile attorney on speed dial, and a couple of judges in his pocket." He squinted at the screen and bit his lip. "We go by the book on this case."

"It's not just any case. My partner and her sister are in there with a deranged lunatic." James bolted up but miscalculated the van's dimensions and cracked his head. "Mother ... argh." James pounded his fist on the van wall. "Dammit! This falls under exigent circumstances. *Fuck* your warrant!"

O'Malley yanked off his headset and stood hunched, meeting his friend's eyes. "Would you care to repeat that, Agent Powers?"

James exhaled and wiped the sweat from his forehead. "Sorry. My emotions are running high on this one."

"That's precisely why you're not on the entry team." He looked at James's thigh. "Jeezo, not to mention, you're bleeding out in my freakin' van, man." He tossed James a roll of paper towels. "Let me call our medic. He's on standby." O'Malley glanced at the spreading blood on James's pants. "I'm sure he has something for that."

"I got it." James removed the first aid kit from his black FBI embossed duffel bag.

"That's right, you were a *Boy Scout*." O'Malley gave him a snarky glance and sat again. "You really saw that son of a bitch get chomped by a gator?"

"Yup, I'd like to erase it from my memory." He dropped his pants and wrapped the gauze a few times around his leg.

"James. I promise, they will be okay. We'll get 'em back. But before we kick in the door, we need confirmation Saki is there."

"Rose said she recognized the boatshed *and* we have exigent circumstances. What are you waiting for?" The blue veins in James's neck protruded.

"Rose has not confirmed that, besides … there's something I need tell you. I've been working this case for a year and—" O'Malley leaned back and crossed his arms. "Max hasn't been able to unload the paintings due to their high notoriety. So, he was looking to trade them on the black market for stolen firearms."

"Wait a minute! We let my partner walk right in the middle of a freakin' arms deal? Are you nuts?"

"*No.* There was chatter the meet and greet was next week. SWAT was gonna get their weapons, and I was going to recover the art pieces. But the abduction changed that a bit. This residence was not even on our radar. It's in his mother's maiden name. Max never transferred it."

"So, you think this is where he keeps those heisted items? And Rose was your foot in the door." James shook his head and finished wrapping his leg.

"Yep."

James pulled up his pants. "We haven't heard from her … something's wrong. I feel it."

He patted over his heart. "In here."

"Damn brother, you have it bad for Rose, don't you?"

"Oh, God, not like that. Well, maybe Saki." He raised a brow. "No. Rose and I are close, and I love her ... in a sisterly way. I made a promise to my best friend, her late husband, I'd look out for her. And that's exactly what I'm gonna do." He turned to the van's door handle.

"James, Stop!" O'Malley grabbed his hand.

CHAPTER 65

I froze. The last time I saw him our mothers were in the kitchen upstairs making lasagna and laughing. Their merriment turned to screams as they ran to gunshots that echoed from the boatshed where our fathers held their weekly business meeting. But instead of doing shots of whiskey and discussing the future of M.T. Art, a fatal blast changed the course of our lives.

I flashed back to Sammy or Max, whoever he was now.

"Where the fuck is my sister?"

"Wow, such language." Max opened his arms and approached me. "Is that how you greet an old boyfriend?" He wore a cheeky grin.

"Don't come any closer!" My neck felt hot with rage. "Oh, and we—" I waved my finger between us— "were never boyfriend and girlfriend, *Sammy*!" I spit daggers.

His smile faded. He twitched. "I am Max, Sammy does not exist." He responded with a calm, chilling tone.

"Where. Is. Saki?" I shouted, hoping my team would pick up my transmission. "Don't make me ask again."

"You're not making this fun for me." Max drew a heavy, exaggerated sigh. "She's in the boatshed." He glanced at his watch. "But, I'm afraid you're too late."

"What? You told me eight thirty, it's eight. I'm early."

Max walked over and removed a black soundproof panel, exposing a window to the rear property. "You are correct. You're on time for the show." He waved his arm as if he were a ringmaster at a circus. "D.O.G., you're needed."

The giant man marched in and tossed the clown off the chair, shoving me backward on it. I grimaced as his burly arms ripped off my sling and tied my hands behind my back. "I held up my end of the deal. I brought the Falcon." I glared. "Some man you've become. You're a wuss, like when you were a kid."

Max bent over and smacked my cheek.

I kept emotion off my face and fought to sit quietly while the pain surged through my body.

Max brushed a strand of his raven black hair off his forehead that fell out of place during the slap. "You see the boatshed?" He pointed through the double pane hurricane windows. "In about fifteen minutes D.O.G. will call this number." He plucked a cell from his pocket and presented it to me. "And ... kaboom!" He gestured his hands in a blow-up motion as he passed the phone to D.O.G.

Fury descended, fast as a red-hot cloak constricting my throat. *I did not come here to watch my sister die.* "You turned into one twisted, sick mother fucker." I spit through gritted teeth. I stood. "Saki did nothing to you, you son of a bitch!"

If you got no spunk, you're dead, my Grandma Lil once told me. For now, I was still alive and ready to fight.

CHAPTER 66

I hit a nerve. Max twitched and clocked me again. I flew across the room. The blow created a pressure in my skull and buzzing in my ears. Just then I picked up faint radio traffic. I should have thanked him, but gratitude was at the bottom of my list.

"Wussy boy! I thought your mother taught you to never hit a woman." I poked a hibernating bear and had no plans of stopping.

"Pick her up, I don't want her missing a thing."

D.O.G. obeyed and sat me back down. But he didn't notice the restraints loosened during my flight.

"That will be all." Max flicked his wrist and D.O.G. left up the stairs.

Max turned and sucker punched me. The

wind escaped my lungs, and I gasped and pitched forward in my seat.

"Nobody speaks of my deceased mother that way, ever again!"

Breathe, Rose. I sat tall and waited for my abdominal muscles to wake. "We *both* lost our mothers. I don't feel sorry for you, asshole," I wheezed.

He drew his face closer. "*But* the difference is, your father took away mine. She died of a broken heart." The force of his scream blew my hair.

"How the hell were we responsible for his actions? We were children!"

He stepped back. "You left and never returned my letters. We stood right here and promised we would be together ... forever." He wore a far-off stare.

"I didn't leave, they took me away ... and I never got your letters."

He did not hear my words. "You left me with ... with him!" Max shuffled around in a trance and touched the walls. He spoke with a monotone voice.

"Him, who?" I twisted and turned my wrists.

"My step-father! She was forced to marry him after Daddy was killed. He made this room soundproof so no one would hear the weekly beatings. He said it would make me tough, make me a man. He called me a son of a bitch and my mom a whore." Max did not blink.

"He'd tell my mommy I was at a friend's for the weekend, but ... I wasn't. I was here. And no one knew, not even Heidi. That is when

Sammy died. Don't you see, Rosie?" He wore a childlike expression, and his voice softened.

Max was gone.

"Sammy, I'm here now." I lied to distract him. I read about Dissociative Identity Disorder in psychology class. Max's was atypical. He had two, and they were aware of one another.

"Oh, Rosie." He ran over to me. "I am so sorry. Are you all right?"

I studied this damaged man as I struggled to loosen the rope. "It's okay Sammy. Can you untie me? These kinda hurt. I came back so we can play and be tog—"

He closed his eyes and jerked his head. "*No!*" He sprung to his feet and adjusted his shirt. He snapped the rubber band on his wrists and paced. "No, no, no. Sammy is dead!" He pulled it harder and faster.

CHAPTER 67

As I worked on freeing myself, Max was making a comeback. I had to keep Sammy talking.

"I'm sorry, Sammy. What happened?"

"I turned sixteen." He bought it and returned his gaze to mine.

"Mm hm." I stopped and nodded.

"I was bigger and done with the beatings. Then one day I challenged him, knowing he'd hit me harder." He fixed his hair and picked lint from his shirt. Sammy disappeared. "I had to show the cops it was self-defense. I kept him angry and wore him down, and then ..." He pulled off another panel. "I bashed his head in the wall, right here." He pointed to a faint blood stain.

"They sentenced me to eleven months in

juvenile hall. When I got out, I changed my name and had my records sealed. I became Max. Sammy was too weak and ceased to exist ... until you came back into my life."

"Wait a minute! You came looking for me."

"*No*. All I wanted was the Falcon. But, seeing you suffer ... that takes the cake."

Max regained control. "Your sister will die in ..." He looked at his watch. "Eight more minutes."

"I assume you're gonna kill me too?"

"No, you get to live with the pain of watching someone you love die. The way I have." He shot me an icy stare and returned to the window. "Once the pain is gone, Rose, all we have left is hate."

"You weren't the only one with heartache, *Sammy*. But I don't hate."

He spun, and I was out of my chair and in his face.

CHAPTER 68

Saki's heart palpitated as the key crumbled to pieces in her hand. "No, no, no!" She ran to the windows and pushed up with all her strength, but they were jammed shut.

Just then a man emerged from the other side of the shed. "Crockett, Crockett! Please help me. I promise I won't tell anyone. Let me go." Her face was flush against the windows as she pounded.

He ignored her plea and continued to tape the bomb to the door. Sweat poured out of her as the temperature mounted. Her breathing was labored as she scanned the boatshed for something, anything, that would work. She found it in the corner, a hammer and crowbar, and returned to the back door. As she pummeled as hard as her slippery hands would allow, she found the hinge rusted fast. It was useless.

Suddenly, out of the corner of her eye, she saw Crockett bolting for safety.

"*Coward!*" She screamed as loud as she could and threw the chair against the window, breaking it. A light breeze made its way inside, and for a moment she could breathe. Wait ... Saki stood on the chair and smashed out the remaining glass with the hammer, but the windows were too small for her to crawl through. "*God*, no! Please help me," she wailed.

With a heavy spirit, she surrendered to her destiny and returned to the rear exit. Maybe the blast wouldn't be as strong back there. As she dropped to her knee to say the Lord's Prayer, a bulging piece of metal poked through the mat.

She yanked it away and discovered the answer to her prayer: a scuba door.

CHAPTER 69

"**H**arbor Patrol One ... status?" O'Malley demanded in his mic.

"This is Harbor Patrol One. No visual on either woman, but there is activity by the boatshed. Cruising in for a closer peek."

"Copy that ... Harbor Patrol Two?"

"Harbor Patrol Two, there's movement on target's property. His Lamborghini and Stingray departed, stand by ... Porsche, too. They are clearing the vehicles, something's going down."

"Command ... this is Aerial one." A twenty-something-year-old newbie's voice shook from behind his desk in Miami as he maneuvered the drone with the left haptic joystick and gimbal dial on the right.

"Go ahead, Aerial one."

"Sir, there appears to be a male subject attaching a device to the door of the boatshed."

"This is Harbor Patrol One, affirmative, he's taping a cell phone to the outside of the door."

"I need a visual on that device!" O'Malley slammed his hand on the desk.

"Sending it now," Harbor Patrol One replied.

The agents in the florist van shared a wide-eyed glance. "Shit, it's an explosive charge, he's using the cell phone as a remote trigger." As they stooped over in the van, O'Malley shook his head. "It's pretty sophisticated, James."

"This looks like an Al-Qaeda type device," James reported. "You don't think Titos? You know what he did in the military."

"Titos may not have been loyal to his own department, but he was loyal to his country," O'Malley said as they shot a doubting glance at one another. "Maybe Max or one of his goons found it in *Inspire*. AQAP, ya know?"

"Huh?" James tilted his head.

"Al Qaeda in the Arabian Peninsula, they are an affiliate and put this shit on-line for the sick anti-American fuckers."

"Oh, yeah ... those assholes. Wait a minute, what kind of arm's dealer was Max meeting with? He's not—"

"No! That never came up in our investigation." O'Malley crossed his arms and ran his hand over his head.

"I'll bet he has one of those anti-jamming devices too, that's how we lost radio contact with Rose." They stared at the screen.

"And we can't jam the signal without

collateral damage to the 911 com center," O'Malley said.

"Can't we ask them to briefly shut down the cell service in this area?" James bit his fingernail.

O'Malley pulled out his cell, "Already on—"

"This is Harbor Patrol One ... male subject ran from the boatshed."

"Everyone in position. We move now ... O'Brien, do you copy? Get out!" O'Malley ordered.

CHAPTER 70

As he approached, I lowered my center of gravity into a fighting stance. He charged me, and out of instinct, I delivered a left palm-heel strike. It was a colossal mistake. I should have hit with my right. "Fuck!" I clenched my jaw as the stitches ripped for the last time.

I swept his legs from beneath him but underestimated his long extremities. He went down, taking me with him. As I fell, I pulled one out of my toolbox and thrust my good elbow into his solar plexus.

Max sounded like a deflating balloon as the air escaped his body. But with his adrenaline running high, he shook it off. "Give it up, Rosie!" He taunted like a schoolyard bully. "You're no match for me." He grunted. "You were always a weak little girl and you still are."

He had me pinned in a wrestler's sleeper hold.

Weak?! The word seared through my brain like a branding iron. I tucked in my chin, shot my elbows back. "*Argh!*" I let out an immense yell and bolted up, as my Kahr propelled out of my bra holster. He followed suit and jumped to his feet. Our eyes locked, throats tightened, then we spotted the weapon in the corner.

Max was closer and reached it before I did. He drew on me, but I had the upper hand. I was trained at disarming.

I deflected with my bloody left hand, jammed the muzzle into his thigh, and punched his nose. He howled. "You bitch!" I grabbed the butt of the pistol and twisted it out of his grip.

"It's Rose ... that's Agent O'Brien to you, *asshole!*"

I aimed the gun at him. In his rage, he rushed me.

Double tap. Max dropped.

I darted out of the room, up the steps, and out the front door. "Crockett ... cell bomb ... boatshed gonna blow ..." I shouted as I sprinted on the lawn toward my sister, but a member of the team snatched me.

"No, Agent O'Brien, it's not safe. I have ord—"

"No!" I screamed and wiggled free, running as fast as my legs would carry me. I had to get there. I had to be in time. I had to save Saki.

Just as my foot touched the boat dock, *BOOM!*

I hurled backward and faded to flashing red and blue emergency lights.

CHAPTER 71

Déjà vu. A warm peacefulness embraced me as Saki stood by my side. She wore a light pink flowing dress, and a luminous ray shone around her. "Are we in—"

Saki smiled widely and caressed my arm. "Yes, we are Rosie."

"Sorry, Ms. Rose." A short petite nurse whispered as she closed the curtains. "The sunlight is so blinding."

As my vision readjusted, I saw James standing next to Saki, holding her by the waist as she leaned on crutches. Joyful tears trickled down my face. I tried to reach out, but couldn't move.

James set his hand on mine. "How are you feeling, love?"

I examined my body and saw a leg in a cast

and an immobile shoulder. "I am just *fine*." I glanced at Saki, and we chuckled. "I'm actually more than that, I'm fantastic." I couldn't keep my eyes off her. "Honey, I'm sorry for everything."

"Shh." She raised her finger to her mouth. "We'll talk later."

I nodded. "Wait. How did you get out of the boatshed?"

"Heidi ..." Saki scanned the room.

"Oh, she's getting coffee," James said.

"She gave me a key to the back door, but it was rusty and busted. So, I jumped through the scuba door seconds before the explosion. A piece of flying shrapnel cut my leg. It's no biggie, just a few stitches. Luckily, my hero, James." She beamed at him with a twinkle. "Fished me out of the ocean."

"Like a magnificent mermaid." James's pupils dilated and cheeks were rosy.

"Okay, wait a minute. How long was I out for this time? There is obviously something going on between you two."

Saki and James held each other's gazes. "Most definitely," they answered in unison, then chuckled. "Jinx!" Saki said.

James turned to me. "You have been out a week, love. They put you in a medically induced coma because of the swelling on your stubborn brain." He kissed my forehead.

"That's why I have a massive headache." I snort laughed.

"She's baaack!" Saki giggled.

"Hey, what about Max? Is he—"

"I can answer that one, Red," Agent O'Malley said as he entered.

CHAPTER 72

O'Malley stood in the doorway with a bouquet of roses mixed with lilies and baby's breath and placed them on the table with some other get-well offerings. O'Malley gave me a cheeky grin. His features were relaxed.

"Thank you ... so thoughtful. Roses are my favorite." I grinned back.

O'Malley and I locked eyes and he cleared his throat. "Uh, anyway, to answer your question, Max is not dead. The bastard made a run for it."

"He did what? But, how? I shot him!"

"During our surveillance, Max's Master Craft sped off, with just the captain on board. We let him go. But right after you ran out the front door, we spotted D.O.G. helping him to his

Airbus H175. It was hiding in plain sight. They got away, this time. As to being shot, he hasn't been to any hospital, so either it was superficial, or he's got a doctor on his payroll."

"How'd he find out about the raid?" I asked.

James chimed in. "An inside leak. Titos was not the only one on his staff. He also had a nurse who worked at the local jail. She caught wind of our operation." He shook his head.

"Yep, they bailed, but thanks to you, we recovered the Vermeer and a couple more." O'Malley winked.

"Is there a finder's fee, Kevin?" James laughed. "You know, Rose is back to the working wages of a parole agent since she gave Max the Falcon."

"Are you sure about that?" Kaylee walked in the room.

CHAPTER 73

Our eyes were trained on Kaylee as she stopped in the doorway. James's mouth hung open as he shot glances at the three of us, while O'Malley stood silent and looked more confused than everyone.

"Let's just say the Falcon is in protective custody." I snorted, breaking the awkward silence.

"But we heard you give it to D.O.G.," James said.

I wore a Cheshire grin as Kaylee stood at my bedside. "I gave it to someone for safekeeping."

"Whoa, wait a minute. No offense to you." Saki put her palm to Kaylee and turned back to me. "But how the hell did you, of all people, trust a complete stranger with a five-million-dollar painting?"

"Um, Saki, you better sit for this one ... I want you to meet our half-sister, Kaylee."

"Uh ... wha ...?" Saki hobbled backwards on her crutches and plopped on her chair.

"I thought you looked familiar." James blurted as he eased down next to Saki.

After Kaylee recounted our story, she said she had no interest in money from the Falcon. Saki and I disagreed, she was family. Any profit from the Falcon should be shared equally.

"I have a question, ladies." Saki broke her silence. "Is he still alive?"

Kaylee shrugged.

While my sisters got acquainted, I tuned out and stared at an unusual flower arraignment. The nursing staff informed me an elderly man brought them while I was in the coma. They said he held my hand and talked to me every night after my other visitors left.

My evening nurse, Risse, told me he had "a sad gentleness to him." Since I had no visitor restrictions, she took pity on him and allowed him to stay past hours. Two nights ago, Risse unintentionally eavesdropped and overheard him apologizing to me.

I smiled as I gazed at the large red rose surrounded by smaller yellow, pink, and orange ones, and knew the answer to Saki's question.

CHAPTER 74

A week earlier.

"D.O.G., Crockett, we are home free. The feds seized most of my U.S. assets, but I still have my foreign holdings, a villa in Sardinia, among others." Max laid back on his chaise longue on the top deck of his 87-foot, 186 Delta superyacht, with helipad and boat garage. He offered his face to the sun and sipped his dry martini.

"Uh, and your health," Lucy chimed in as she finished bandaging his torso. "You're lucky she missed your vital organs."

Max shrugged and waved his empty glass in the air.

Just then Crockett came up from the lower deck. "Don't forget this too, boss. It's worth a few million. It should buy us a couple more planes." He laughed and set it on the serving table.

"Ahh, yes. You can say the Falcon completes me, but it's not for sale. It has more than monetary value, my friend. Much more."

Max shuffled over, holding his stomach. "Let's have a look, Croc." He removed the layers of wrapping and stood back. "What the *hell* is this?!" Max shouted at the pastel painting of the Florida landscape that should be in a hotel lobby, not in his private gallery.

A note fell out and floated to the deck.

Don't worry, you will be just F.I.N.E.

"*Son of a bitch!*"

THE END
MAYBE

AUTHORS NOTE

As a dog lover, I wanted to pay homage to my two fur babies, Saki and Rose. Instead of writing about dogs, I chose to bring them to the human world. Most of the characters in this story are loosely based on Saki's and Rose's K-9 friends. This story is dedicated to all present, past, and future fur babies. I hope you enjoy.

List of characters and their K-9 identities.

Rose

Saki

Kaylee

Titos

D.O.G.   Crockett

Tubbs   Heidi

Daisy   Scarlett

Lucy

Max, a lab mix,
was a childhood pet.
Picture unavailable.

ABOUT THE AUTHOR

S.S. Duskey retired from law enforcement with over 20 years of experience. She resides in the Bitterroot Mountains of Montana with her husband, Steve, and fur baby, Rose. Rose and her late canine companion, Saki, are Sharon's inspirations for writing, not to mention her adventures throughout her career.

When she is not plotting mischief for her characters, Sharon enjoys spending time with her family, friends, and furry children in the outdoors of the beautiful Bitterroot.

She invites you to visit her face book page S.S. Duskey, or contact her via e-mail at ssduskey@yahoo.com .

Made in United States
Troutdale, OR
03/20/2024

18601257R00130